A YULETIDE HIGHLANDER

Highland Heather Romancing a Scot: Castle Brides

Book Ten

Collette Cameron®

Attn: Permissions Coordinator
Blue Rose Romance® LLC
info@collettecameronbooks.com
eBook ISBN: 978-1-954307-92-6
Print Book ISBN: 978-1-955259-93-4
collettecameronbooks.com

FREE BOOK!

JOIN MY EXCLUSIVE MAILING LIST
Collette Cameron Newsletter

AND GET A FREE EBOOK!

https://collettecameronbooks.com/freegift

Plus Sneak Peeks, Giveaways, Contests, Exclusive Content, and More... P.S. I promise only good stuff ~ **no** spam!

Contents

Acknowledgments

A very special thanks to Maryann Dixon Mosby for suggesting Stinkwiggon's name, and to my entire VIP Group, Collette's Chéris for selecting *A Yuletide Highlander's* title. I know I can always count on you for excellent feedback.

Thanks to my awesome assistant DF for keeping me sane, and never grumbling when I sent her last minute requests so that I could keep writing *A Yuletide Highlander*. This was my first fully dictated book, and I completed it in ten days. That's not to say there wasn't a great deal of rewriting when the recorder decided gibberish was better than what I spoke. Still, with a hand healing from surgery, I am extremely grateful for dictation programs.

Finally, because you asked for Gregor McTavish's story, over and over, I must give credit to you, my loyal readers for not giving up, for your enduring patience, and for your continued encouragement.

~

Dedication

To every one of my dear readers who are missing a loved one this Yuletide season.
Sending you hugs, prayers, and comforting thoughts.

ONE

East India Docks, London England

December 1826

The oak entry to Stapleton Shipping and Supplies flew open, and a wet young man bolted inside, his chest rising and falling as he gasped for breath. Panic pinched his thin face as he swiftly shut the door behind him. He grasped a small blade wedged into the worn leather belt encircling his navy bridge coat as his frightened gaze careened from corner to corner of Gregor McTavish's office.

Gregor had seen that same terrified look in the ebony eyes of a fox caught in a snare. Still grasping the quill hovering over his account books, while gripping the dirk he'd yanked from his boot when the youth dashed inside, he relaxed his tense posture.

This scared spitless waif, his back angled toward him while peeking at the pier around the window sash, wasn't a threat. Scrutinizing the dreary, water-soaked gray docks, Gregor lowered the quill while slipping his blade back into his boot.

Rain pelted a trio of burly, unkempt thugs heatedly arguing several yards away. Wrath contorted their apparent leader's face, and he flung a stocky arm toward a narrow alley a block farther along the wharf.

The largest of the other men shook his head, and the brute drove his open hand into the man's chest then smacked the shorter, swarthy-skinned sailor on the side of the head with enough force to send him stumbling backward a few steps.

Fists balled, the other man took a menacing step forward, but the bully puffed out his chest and yelled something. Whatever he said stalled the other man mid-step. After a slight pause and exchanging infuriated glances, his two companions thundered off.

Where to, and why did every instinct suggest the lad would know? Gregor veered a swift, hooded glance toward the boy before refocusing his regard on the sailor.

Only three buildings opened directly onto this section of docks. Was his uninvited visitor fleeing those thugs?

His hands on his hips, a fierce scowl pulling the corners of his eyes and mouth downward, the remaining sailor rotated slowly to the left and then to the right. He obviously searched for something. *Or someone.* His acute gaze swept past Stapleton Shipping and Supplies then slowly gravitated back.

Even from his seat, Gregor recognized the shrewdness quirking the sailor's mouth and gleaming in his narrowed eyes fixated on his office.

His nape prickled.

Danger.

He stood, pushing his unfashionably long hair over his shoulder. In the Highlands, he seldom tied it back, and he oft' forgot to do so in the morning since moving to London almost a year ago. He rather enjoyed the shocked expressions his blond mane caused the stuffy upper echelons of society.

The boy's narrow shoulders and back quaked. From cold or fear?

"Can I help ye?"

The lad spun to face him, his frightened gaze ricocheting about the office once more.

Nae, no' a laddie. A lass. A comely one at that.

"I'm Gregor McTavish." He introduced himself, careful to keep his tone calm and soothing in the hopes he might alleviate some of her fright. "My cousin's wife owns these buildin's and this establishment."

"Those men attempted to abduct me." Still breathing hard, she motioned toward the window. "Might I stay here for a few minutes until the last one leaves?"

"Aye, of course." Brutes, like those outside, had no honorable business with bonnie lasses.

At first glance, because of her height, bulky, dark blue overcoat, and sailor's cap, Gregor had mistaken her for a boy. She wasn't as young as he'd first believed either, though she certainly was not on the shelf. About the ages of his Ferguson step-cousins—somewhere in her early to mid-twenties, he'd guess.

Another inspection of the dock sent alarm, sparking up his spine.

The unsavory fellow tramped across the wooden walkway, straight for Stapleton Shipping.

Damnation.

"Quick, lass. Come here. He's comin'." Gregor made an urgent gesture. "Hide beneath my desk. *Now.*"

In a blink, she dashed across the room, and he stepped back to allow her to crawl into the kneehole.

No sooner had Gregor resumed his seat and dipped his quill in the inkwell than the office door sprang open again. With deliberate intent, he took his time and finished the entry. His mind on the terrified woman crouched inches from his knees, he almost swore upon realizing he'd recorded two hundred and fifty barrels of molasses instead of twenty-five.

The sailor blocking the entry roughly cleared his throat and angrily stamped his feet. The wind blasted rain into the entrance, yet the man made no effort to shut the door.

The blighter earned himself a longer wait. Gregor suppressed a grin and dipped the nib into the ink again.

"Give me a moment," he muttered, taking far longer than a child's first attempt to form the letters of each word. After scribbling a few more lines—he might've ordered more flour than the whole village of Craigcutty could consume in a year —he finished and set the quill aside.

Twisting his mouth into a thin, hard smile, he rested a forearm on the desk and took the blackguard's measure from greasy brown hair, unshaven face and stained clothing, to his even filthier boots. The man's rank odor wafted across the room, and despite the open entry, Gregor's nostrils twitched in protest.

"Come to apply for one of the crew openin's, have ye?" He nonchalantly cradled his jaw in his palm. "Have ye any experience?"

Upon hearing Gregor's Scot's brogue, a sneer curled the man's upper lip. "No. I'm lookin' for a fugitive. She stole a large purse from my employer and was last seen runnin' in this direction."

"Och," Gregor murmured with mock understanding.

The sailor's astute, accusing eyes searched every inch of the office, lingering for a long moment on the half-open door leading to the stairwell and Gregor's apartment. Suspicion flared the man's nostrils before he tore his distrustful scrutiny away.

"I can assure ye, nae lawless lassies have entered this buildin' today." He leaned back and flung a casual look about the tidy office. "As ye can see for yerself," he waved a languid hand, "there's naebody here but Cat and me."

Upon hearing his name, the long-haired white and orange tabby opened his citrine green eyes and yawned, then arched his back before padding over to Gregor and hopping onto the desk. Purring, and with complete disregard for the ledger he stood upon, he pushed his head beneath Gregor's hand, demanding he be petted.

Gregor sliced a pointed look to the open doorway, water dripping from the overhang and wetting the floor.

"If ye'll excuse me." He tapped the ledger with the fingers of his other hand. "I've much work to do. Monthly reports, ye ken. Inventory to take. Supplies to order."

Lasses to protect.

"Receipts to record."

Riddin' my office of stinkin' horses' arses.

"Och, my employer is most demandin'," he rattled on, giving a woeful shake of his head and wholly enjoying the impatience creasing the sea tar's weather-worn face.

Cat, now sprawled full-length across the register, his eyes half-closed in lazy contentment, made a mockery of Gregor's claim he'd work to attend.

He'd rescued the starving kitten from the hard life of a wharf cat after he first arrived in London. Loneliness had compelled him, though he'd never admitted as much to a soul. For the first time in his life, there wasn't the pleasant chaos of a dozen or more people around at any given moment.

The spoiled beast didn't hesitate to show his gratitude. Although at times, his affection embarrassed Gregor. Cat lazily lifted a paw and patted his hand as if to say, "I require your attention. A belly scratch, if you please."

"Nae, I'll no' be rubbin' yer belly." He gathered the cat, frowning at the smudged entries, and placed the ball of sharp-clawed fluff on the floor.

With a dismissive flick of his impossibly long tail, and a few fresh ebony ink stains accenting his silky coat, Cat sauntered to the stairs.

When the man continued to lurk in the doorway, Gregor summoned his most formidable look. The one that usually sent men scuttling away.

"Yer sure I canna talk ye into applyin' for a position? I have a ship sailin' to Africa in a fortnight that needs hands." He scratched the back of his head, raking his gaze up and down the man's form. "Can ye cook?"

The sailor's mouth skewed into another wide sneer, revealing missing, broken, and yellowed teeth. He folded dirty fingers, one by one, around the bone knife hilt protruding from his belt and, spreading his legs, ticked his chin upward as brutes of his ilk were wont to do when bent on threatening others.

"You best be tellin' me the truth, you bloody Scot." He settled another doubtful look on the stairs.

Bloody Scot?

Was the man a lackwit that he dared come in here and hurl insults? This Sassenach piece of horse shite had just tipped the scales from patience to annoyance.

The sailor wasn't a puny weakling, but Gregor and his twin had been called giants on more than a few occasions. And for good reason. Standing well over six and a half feet and massively built, even at three and thirty, no man had ever bettered him in a physical challenge—except for his twin.

Only because of the terrified young woman huddled beneath his desk had he kept a tight rein on his temper and tongue. Otherwise, this codpiece would've already found himself sprawled on the dock—unconscious and arse up.

"Cap'n Santano doesn't take kindly to people interferin' in his business," the blighter pressed.

Why wasn't Gregor surprised to learn this sod worked for Santano?

The captain's nefarious reputation preceded him, and six months ago, Stapleton Shipping and Supplies had refused his request to enter into a commercial relationship. Infuriated and full of his own self-importance, Santano had taken his business elsewhere.

Leisurely rising, and wholly unrepentant, Gregor used his immense size to intimidate the churl. He spoke slowly and deliberately as if addressing a simpleton. "If I tell ye nae thief entered this establishment, then nae thief is here." He made a show of lifting his clenched fists waist-high. "Do ye ken?"

The shady fellow's eyes shifted back and forth several times, and he nervously fingered his scraggy tobacco-stained beard with one hand while the other flexed upon his knife handle. He gave a grudging nod, his bluster disappearing in the face of someone capable of pounding his ugly face into pulp.

"Well, if you do see a tall, skinny blonde wearin' a peacoat, notify the cap'n at once." He half-turned and examined the pier. "While in port, he's usually aboard the *Mary Elizabeth*, at the Seven Seas Alehouse or," a lewd smile curved his mouth. "Madam Mionnet's."

Ah, the infamous brothel. No man valuing his ballocks sampled those whores. Most were fraught with disease.

"The chit usually has a scrawny, crippled whelp with her, about this tall." Santano's henchmen raised his hand midriff high. "You'd best take care, or she and that street rat will pick your pockets clean."

Gregor remained silent as he maneuvered around the corner of the desk. In about thirty seconds, he'd toss the bloody bugger out the door. Mustering what scant patience he had left, he managed to keep his annoyance from showing. "What's yer name, sailor, in case I needed to reach ye?"

"Yeates." After spearing him another hostile glare, he left, not bothering to shut the door behind him.

"Bloody rotter." Gregor closed the door, and though it was only just after two in the afternoon, turned the key in the lock and slid the bolt home, as well.

Rustling alerted him to his fugitive's intention.

"Stay where ye are. He's still watchin' the buildin'. I'm nae sure he believed me when I said ye weren't here, lass."

Her sharp intake of breath revealed she believed her appearance had fooled him into thinking she was a male. Hadn't she glanced in a looking glass of late?

He made a pretense of adjusting the three model ships displayed in the bay window then rearranged a telescope and a couple of maps before turning away.

"Have you a back entrance?" Refinement, but not the haughty cold tone of privileged nobles, colored her voice.

"Aye, but I think ye should stay here for an hour or two."

Or longer.

Gregor placed a sextant atop one of the maps and then, for good measure, added an open compass, positioned just so. Standing back, hands on his hips, he admired his handiwork. *No' bad.*

"You don't understand. My brother's out there. Alone and scared." On all fours, she peeked 'round the side of his desk, a few fair tendrils dangling on either side of her face.

Cleaned up and with a bit of meat on her bones, she'd be a right bonnie lassie.

He bent and flicked a couple of dead flies from the windowsill. Brushing his hands on his trousers, he casually turned halfway around. "Where is he?"

"I left him hiding amongst some barrels outside the cooper's." She jerked her head in that direction. "I attracted those ruffians' attention to lure them away."

One eye on the marina, Gregor ran a hand over his jaw. "I dinna believe ye stole anythin', so why are they after ye?"

At once, a shuttered expression masked her pale face. She pulled her soft mouth into a tight line and fixed her attention on the floor, her gold-tipped lashes fanning her hollow cheeks. Her short nails dug into the floor said what she feared to.

She didn't trust him.

Gregor couldn't blame her, and compassion welled behind his ribs. Survival on London's unforgiving streets meant never trusting anyone.

He eyed her covertly from beneath half-closed eyes. What dire circumstances had forced her and her brother to this life? He hadn't a doubt she'd not been born into it. Everything about her so far suggested she came from a genteel background.

There were few things he liked more than solving a challenging mystery, and this young woman was a puzzle, to be sure. Och...a good fight was always enjoyable, but on occasion, he preferred using his brains rather than brute strength. Only on occasion, mind you.

On hands and knees, the lass edged to the room's farthest corner before scrambling to her feet. Wise on her part. No one outside could see her in the lengthening shadows.

Since becoming his cousin-in-law Yvette McTavish's manager for her London warehouses, his life had been nothing short of mind-numbingly dull. He'd only accepted the position because he was ready—*och, bloody damn desperate*—to do something, anything, different than continuing at Craiglocky Keep, his cousin's castle.

Until just short of a year ago, Craiglocky was the only place Gregor had ever lived, and his sole purpose had been to serve his laird, Ewan McTavish. He'd loved both, still did, but discontentment ate away at him, growing and growing and growing...

Except for him, everyone at the Keep had married. And truthfully, he left as much to escape his extended family's matchmaking attempts as to try his hand at something new. At one time, he thought to become a doctor, and he still dabbled in the healing arts from time to time when called upon to do so. But there hadn't been any real need for his services after Yvette commissioned the building of a local hospital.

Gregor had also believed he'd marry Lily Ellsworth, but several years ago, she'd fallen in love with another. He hadn't been altogether shocked to realize he wasn't heartbroken. She'd been too young for him, in any event. Feeling much older than he was, he'd decided to leave the Highlands for a time.

Someday, he'd return. Scotland was as much a part of him as the blood tunneling through his veins at this very moment. He missed the fragrant heather, the craggy rocks, the hairy cattle, and the bright green meadows. He even preferred the Highland's harsh, unforgiving weather to London's perpetual stench and coal-laden skies.

"Mr. McTavish, I must find my brother right away. He'll be frightened." A tinge of fear peppered her impatience.

"Aye, lass, of course ye do. I'm just thinkin'." Not about rescuing her brother, but what he'd chosen to leave behind. Those musings were a waste of time, and before him was an opportunity to relieve the tedium his life had become as well as to help someone in desperate need. "We canna be too careful with the likes of those blackguards."

She muttered something unintelligible but which sounded distinctly unflattering.

One hand on his hip, he pulled his ear, trying to read her. He'd likely regret becoming involved, but if it brought a dose of excitement into his existence, well, damn it, it'd be worth it.

"Ye can wait upstairs and have yerself somethin' to eat while I fetch yer brother."

Arms folded, she eyed him warily. "Why should I trust you?"

Two

Gregor raised his eyebrows and shoulders at the same time.

"Och, as I see it," he perused the street again, "ye haven't any choice. Ye either accept my aide or take yer chances out there." He jabbed a thumb toward the window. "Need I remind, ye, lass, ye bolted in here on yer own accord?"

Her high cheekbones standing out against her pale skin, she gave a terse nod. "I'd heard good things about Stapleton Shipping and Supplies. That they were honest and fair. I'd hoped someone here would help me."

"Aye, ye made a wise decision." Yeates was right about one thing. She was too thin. "Now, tell me. What does yer brother look like? What's he wearin'?"

"Kipp has dark blond hair and hazel eyes. He has on clothing similar to mine." Gregor would bet all the supplies in the warehouses and every drop of whisky in Scotland that wasn't the boy's real name.

He slipped an arm into his caped greatcoat. He'd go out the front door and draw away anyone watching the building. He eyed the wet floor. It would have to wait until he returned.

"I'll try to find the lad and bring him back here." He stuffed his other arm inside the cumbersome garment. He'd rather don his tartan, but while in Rome and all that…"What's somethin' only he would ken, so he believes ye sent me to fetch him?"

Staying in the shadows, she scratched her temple and blew out a resigned sigh. "Kipp's… He's…" Her voice trailed off.

Gregor glanced up from wrestling with his buttons. "He's what?"

"He's…um…slow mentally and can become easily confused." A challenge shone in her eyes. "He walks with a limp, and running is difficult for him."

"Aye. It's good ye told me." That was why she'd left her brother behind. He'd have been caught for sure. Gregor would need a wagon then. "What's yer name, lass?"

"I'm Sydney Blanes."

He stifled a snort. Not her real name, either. Who was she? What had her so terrified? Och, he'd learn the truth. All in good time.

She pulled the atrocious hat from her head, and a cascade of blonde hair as light as his tumbled to beyond her shoulders.

Momentarily speechless—not typical at all—he forced his attention away. Odin's teeth. She was exquisite. He pointed to the door leading to the stairwell. "As I said, help yerself to any food ye find upstairs. My cat's name is Cat."

Snorting again, loud and mockingly, she shoved the hair off her face. "Thought long and hard about that clever moniker, I'll vow, Highlander."

Was she teasing him?

"I suppose ye'd have picked Fluffy, or Pumpkin, or Cinnamon, or some other undignified name?"

"No." She shook her head, that sunny cascade swinging about her shoulders. "He looks like a Marmalade."

Marmalade? Nae.

Cat would be most offended.

Marmalade was sweet, and Cat most certainly was no'.

Fighting a grimace, he put on his beaver top hat. Blast, but he preferred a tam. That sensible covering at least kept his head warm.

Laird, how he missed wearing a leather vest and woolen kilt or trews, not all this refined popinjay falderol. Still, he'd chosen to leave the Highlands and become a proper man of business. These foppish trappings were part of the sacrifices he'd opted to make.

Yvette had been most adamant he couldn't parade about Stapleton Shipping and Supplies—or London, for that matter —bare-arsed, wearing a kilt, with a sword strapped to his hip and a dirk shoved in his boots, more was the pity. Nothing short of the archangel Gabriel appearing and demanding he do so would induce Gregor to forgo his dirk, however.

Withdrawing a key from his pocket, he wielded the iron toward the back entrance.

"That door's bolted from within, and I'll lock this one. Ye'll be safe as long as ye stay out of sight." Fastening the last button of his greatcoat, he canted his head. "Lass, I'll have yer word ye'll be here when I return. Dinna do somethin' foolish and go off on yer own. Santano has an ugly reputation."

Indecision warred in her eyes. Her situation was precarious either way. Forced to trust a complete stranger or risk being seen and apprehended by Santano's thugs when she tried to find her brother.

"What if someone comes in?" she asked, surprisingly pragmatic.

"Unlikely, but as I said, my cousin-in-law owns this establishment." He flicked a finger toward the window. "And several ships in yonder harbor, as well. Anyone who has a key can be trusted. Now, what can I say to yer brother that he'll ken ye sent me?"

"Tell Kipp..., tell him Satan found us."

Gregor paused in pulling on his gloves, one eyebrow arched to his hairline. She wasn't dafty, was she? "*Satan?*"

For the first time, her mouth curled into some semblance of a smile, and he found himself staring once more. A man could fall in love with that smile. That face.

"Yes, Mr. McTavish. Satan. That's what we call Santano—the man who commandeered our father's ship, the *Mary Elizabeth* and is responsible for our parents' deaths."

SARAH PAINE HESITATED at the top of the stairs, still wondering if she'd made the right decision in trusting Gregor McTavish. For certain, she wasn't ready to reveal her real name to him as yet. Drawing a fortifying breath, she pushed the handle opening the door to his apartment.

Cat—*absurd name for a pet*—brushed past her before disappearing through one of the four doorways leading off the common room. The entire floor must be McTavish's private living quarters. Clearly, a man's abode, for no signs of a feminine touch met her scrutiny, she stepped into a large, open-beamed room lined by windows on the far wall.

She hadn't even thought to ask if he was married. Relief swept her that no angry or confused wife met her on the stoop, demanding to know who she was and what she thought she was doing.

Two russet-toned wingback chairs and a braided rag rug sat before a cozy, blue-and-white tiled unlit fireplace. On the wall opposite the windows, a sofa, along with two side tables, formed a neat row. A painting of what must be the Scottish Highlands hung above the tobacco-brown brocade sofa.

At first glance, she'd assumed the Scot a Dane or Norseman—possibly a fierce Viking descendent. Actually, she'd thought him conceivably the most powerfully-built man she'd ever seen. Mayhap one of the most attractive, too.

No mayhap about it.

Ludicrous.

Sarah gave herself a severe mental shake. She'd no business noticing such things when she literally feared for her life. Head angled, she studied the fairly-decent painting, the only decoration of any kind displayed in the room. Did the great blond Highlander pine for his homeland?

That she well understood, for not a day passed that she wasn't homesick for the tropical island where she and Christopher, her brother's real name, had been born. Truth to tell, she missed the vibrant turquoise ocean, the heavily-scented blossoms, and the bright green yellow-billed parrots, but little else.

Most especially not the snakes, spiders, crocodiles, and insufferable humidity.

Head still tilted, she studied the rugged emerald landscape so very different than Jamaica. Each held an entirely different type of beauty, neither more nor less appealing than the other.

Melancholy engulfed her.

Would she ever see her homeland again?

Yes. She must. There was unfinished business there.

Chilled, she folded her arms and circled the room, impressed by its neatness.

Why she'd expected otherwise, she wasn't sure. Perchance because Papa and Chris weren't particularly tidy.

The office below had been organized, and except for two stacks of paper on a narrow table behind McTavish's desk, nothing lay strewn or stacked about. Stapleton Shipping and Supplies had an estimable reputation, and that—along with a great deal of desperation—had prompted her to bolt inside as she fled Santano's henchmen.

Her stomach growled and cramped, reminding her she

and Chris hadn't eaten since fleeing their lodgings down the back stairwell yesterday morning. Barely escaping at that.

Poor, sweet Chris.

He'd been asking for something to eat all morning.

How had Santano found them after all this time? Had she grown careless? Pressing two fingertips between her eyebrows, she closed her eyes and reflected back over the past few weeks.

No. She hadn't.

More likely, her landlord couldn't resist a bribe. Knowing Santano's thugs as she did, the hardly-more-than-a-closet-room she and Chris had called home for the past few months had undoubtedly been ransacked.

There'd be no returning. Not even to collect their meager belongings.

Three years ago, when calamity befell her parents, with nowhere else to go, and scared witless, they'd arrived in England. At once, although she'd never met them, Sarah sought her maternal grandparents, the Viscount and Viscountess Rolandson, at their London house.

The self-important butler had coolly taken their measure from gaunt faces to soiled and wrinkled clothing. With a sneer curling his thin lips and elevating his hooked nose, he'd looked down upon them as if they smelled of pond scum or horse excrement and flatly refused them admittance. After announcing with a peculiar, haughty glee that Lord Rolandson had been dead a decade.

They *had* smelled, and Sarah flushed in renewed humiliation.

When she'd attempted to press her point, and insisted she be allowed to speak to her grandmother, she'd been informed in no uncertain terms that she and Chris were to remove themselves at once. The dowager viscountess had no wish to see them, and if they dared to show their unwelcome persons again, the authorities would be called.

It seemed Grandmother Rolandson hadn't forgiven her gentle-bred daughter for refusing to marry the stuffy English lord her parents had selected for her. That explained the unopened letters returned to Mama over the years.

One of the few times Mama had spoken of her childhood, she'd mentioned the grand house she'd been raised in and which was unentailed. The mansion was settled upon the viscountess by her father when she wed. For whatever reason, Mama said, her mother preferred the house over the viscounty property in Mayfair.

Her mother rarely spoke of her elopement with Papa or her privileged upbringing. She'd never once complained about the long months Papa spent away sailing or about the hardships of living in the tropics.

In fact, Sarah had only discovered her grandmother's address when she opened the satchel Mama had stuffed into her hands as she ordered her and Chris to run and not turn back. Several letters, along with jewels, money, and a few other essential documents, lay inside the bag. She hadn't even been confident the dowager viscountess would be in residence.

Sarah gripped the hidden pocket she'd sewn into her trousers. Eyes closed, she rubbed her cheek against the sturdy wool collar of her coat. Papa's coat. His scent had long since disappeared, but the durable outerwear withstood England's harsh rain, wind, and cold.

The pocket she clutched held what few jewels and coins remained, and a couple of documents wrapped in leather, one of which was the deed of purchase for the *Mary Elizabeth*. The pouch contained a key as well, and she'd long suspected that was what Santano sought.

Even with her eyes tightly closed, Sarah couldn't block the memory of that awful day when her life crumbled apart.

"Find Captain Pritchard," Mama had ordered. "Tell him your father was right, and Santano's have commandeered the

Mary Elizabeth. The captain will see you and Chris safely to England. The arrangements have all been made, my darling."

Her parents must've suspected Santano would betray Papa.

"No, Mama," Sarah had wept. "I cannot leave you."

THREE

Weak as she had been, Mama had taken Sarah by the shoulders and kissed her forehead.

"You must, my darling girl. I don't believe Santano is above killing you and your brother. I shall only slow you down, and we both know my health is too fragile to travel. Now go, and always remember how much your father and I love you. Take care of Chris. He'll need you more than ever now."

A lone tear dribbled slowly over Sarah's cheek, and she hastily swiped it away.

For over three years she and Chris had hidden in the seedier parts of London, moving frequently, and using false names. She'd avoided the docks and other areas where sailors were wont to roam, except for a weekly visit to a street urchin to learn if the *Mary Elizabeth* had laid anchor.

Twice, she'd learned the ship had put into port. The emaciated waif spying on her behalf earned a half-penny for his efforts and an extra for keeping silent about her inquiries. But last week, a wicked cough had kept Chris abed, and she hadn't been able to query about ship arrivals.

The one time she hadn't checked in all these long months, blister it, and Santano had slithered ashore. Eyes and fists squeezed hard, Sarah, released a frustrated groan. Despite all of her efforts, she hadn't been careful enough.

Santano. The despicable rotter.

He'd been father's closest friend, his first officer aboard the *Mary Elizabeth.* Until greed and thirst for power had overcome him, and the fiend had convinced other spineless traitors to mutiny. Everyone who'd stood with Papa now lay dead on the bottom of the Atlantic Ocean.

At least that's the story Sarah had parceled together.

With a ragged breath, she shook off her morose musings. There was nothing she could do about the past. *Yet.* For now, she must concentrate her efforts on avoiding Santano.

Taking a quick peek into the other four rooms, she discovered a kitchen area, two bedrooms, and what appeared to be a good-sized storage closet. Cat had made himself comfortable on one of the main room's windowsills, and one striped leg pointed ceilingward, was engaged in a thorough grooming session.

Her stomach complained loudly again, and Sarah yielded to her hunger, cutting a thin slice of delicious-smelling brown bread and a small piece of hard cheese.

Standing off to the side of the multi-paned windows, she nibbled her simple meal and surveyed the wharf. Dock laborers rushed to and fro as wagons and carts laden with all manner of goods rumbled in both directions, first delivering products and then carting others away.

She shivered, her wet, woolen coat offering little warmth. Would she ever become accustomed to the damp grayness that shrouded England and penetrated her bones? How she longed for the Caribbean's fresh air, colorful flowers, and bird calls.

Naturally, now that Santano had found her, she'd have to leave London. Immediately.

The bread she'd been chewing dried on her tongue, but a wry smile curved her mouth. Where could she go? Strangers, especially a cripple, would draw unwanted attention in the villages and smaller towns.

She had lived frugally these past three years, but little of the money Mama had sent remained. Even before her grandmother had turned them away, she'd been afraid to seek employment. It was too easy to track her. Besides, she couldn't leave Chris alone while she worked. And the truth of it was, she possessed no skill beyond an average education that might gain her a respectable position.

A gust of wind splattered raindrops against the windowpanes, and careful to remain out of sight, she searched for any sign of Chris or Gregor McTavish. He hadn't been gone long, but neither was the cooper's very far.

There was no help for it. She must swallow her pride, temper her misgivings, and ask the giant Scot to help her leave London and mayhap find employment in her new local. Though why or how he'd do so, she couldn't fathom.

They were strangers, after all. But for whatever reason, she trusted the Highlander.

Over the years, she'd learned to rely on gut instinct above all else. And the plain, ugly truth was, she had no choice but to put her faith in him. Nevertheless, she didn't like it one jot.

Popping the last morsel of cheese into her mouth, she scowled.

What was taking the Scot so long?

She bent forward, squinting at the docks, and several strands of lanky hair swung forward. While running from Santano's men, she'd lost the ribbon tying it back. Her hair, in desperate need of washing, had dried in straggly tendrils. She flipped the strands over her shoulder, longing for days past when a warm, scented bath was the norm and not a wishful luxury.

When clean and her stomach full, she'd been able to sleep through the night without fear of someone breaking into their room. She'd taken to wearing men's clothing a scant fortnight after setting foot in England after continually being approached by men in search of female company.

It was a wonder, really, that she hadn't been set upon or despoiled. The knife at her waist acted as a detriment to the less bold.

Her stomach tightened again, but not from hunger. She couldn't see the cooper's from here, but surely Gregor been able to find Chris by now. Unless Santano's goons had...

She tamped down the unthinkable notion. Chris was just hiding. She'd taught him well, and much like a fawn hidden by a doe, he'd learned not to budge until Sarah returned for him.

Another overloaded wagon rumbled through a puddle, its wheels spraying dirty water to the sides, and she bit her lip.

Should she go look for Chris herself?

No, confound it.

She'd given her word she'd stay here. So stupid, to have entrusted him to a stranger.

Gregor had promised he'd find him. If she wasn't here, and he returned with Chris, her brother would panic for sure. He didn't deal well with change, and he'd grown progressively weaker these past months.

Twelve years his senior, Sarah had been thrilled when Mama delivered the skinny, sickly babe. His birth had been difficult, and for the first several weeks, they'd feared he'd die. Another couple of stressful months passed before anyone realized he'd never be quite normal.

As she'd told Gregor, Chris's was a trifle slow mentally, and his right leg dragged when he walked. His right arm bent slightly inward toward his torso, as well. But he was sweet and kind, and Sarah adored him. He was her beloved brother.

She'd promised Mama to keep him safe and never to leave him, and she meant to keep that vow.

He was also the rightful heir to Bellewood House and the *Mary Elizabeth*, and someday, somehow, she'd see his inheritance restored to him or the properties sold and the monies used to ensure he never wanted for anything. And if she ever married—not likely, but not impossible—her husband would have to agree to allow Chris to live with them. Always.

With one eye on the wharf as she awaited Gregor's return, she fingered the outline of the key hidden at her waist.

Did Santano truly know about the chest hidden in Bellewood's cellars? He must, but how had he come by the knowledge? As far as Sarah was aware, only she and her parents knew of its existence.

One time, about a year after Chris's birth, Papa had shown her a hidden chamber behind a rock wall beneath the house's main floor. Hardly more substantial than the pantry, he'd made her swear to tell no one about the small room.

The hidey-hole contained a locked mid-sized chest, a few leather packets, several small coin pouches—which Mama had given her when Sarah fled Jamaica—two elaborate gold chalices as well as a few jewels.

At the time, Sarah hadn't questioned why Papa had revealed the hidden chamber. He'd made it clear because of Chris's mental and physical shortfalls, her brother would require care his entire life. The hideaway's contents were to be used toward that end.

As an adult nearing her fifth and twentieth birthday, Sarah now suspected Papa mightn't have come by the items entirely honestly, and she never learned precisely what the chest contained. Pirates and privateers anchored in Port Royal by the dozens in the seventeenth century.

Had Papa found a buried treasure on Bellewood House's property?

Or had he come by it another way?

She'd likely never know.

It was difficult to reconcile the idea that the kind man who seldom raised his voice in anger could've also been a buccaneer or privateer. If he had been, Santano, as his first mate, surely would've known about any treasure.

The window had grown steamy from her face nearly pressed to the cold glass, and Sarah drew away a few inches.

Once, when she'd been eighteen years old, she'd broached the subject of the room and its contents with her mother. Even then, Mama's constitution had been delicate. For as much as she loved her husband and enjoyed living in the tropics, neither the heat nor the insects suited her.

Her mother had given her a gentle smile, and after kissing Sarah on the forehead, patted her cheek. "Don't worry your pretty head about it, my dear. When the time is right, you'll know all. You know your father is a man of integrity, and he has ensured that long after he and I are gone, you'll never have to worry about how to care for your brother."

Sarah gave the hidden bag a hard squeeze.

She was exhausted—tired of running and living in fear, and yes, saddened, that her only living relative refused to acknowledge them. Mama claimed the Rolandsons' pride would be their downfall.

Sarah had hoped that time would have healed her grandparents' disappointment. But her grandfather had gone to his grave, a bitter curmudgeon, and her grandmother's reputation as a demanding, cantankerous snob was whispered about even amongst the lower orders.

Lady Rolandson also wasn't aware her daughter had died.

Scorching tears stung behind Sarah's eyes, and her heart twisted with grief.

Had Mama died?

There'd been no way to correspond with her.

The only person she'd trusted to deliver a letter had been Captain Pritchard. His ship had sunk shortly after he'd seen her and Chris safely to London. All hands had been lost, and Mama wouldn't be able to write her without an address.

No, if Mama were alive, she'd have written the viscountess. But given the many returned letters over the years, the effort would've been in vain.

"Grandmother, how can you be so cold-hearted?" she asked aloud. "Have you no desire to meet your grandchildren? To know what became of your only daughter?"

Mayhap Sarah would try one last time to contact her grandmother.

Gregor might be persuaded to deliver a letter on her behalf. If Lady Rolandson still refused to see her, then she'd make no attempt to contact the woman again. Right now, the most important thing was keeping Chris safe and escaping Santano's clutches.

Exhausted to the marrow of her bones, she rested her forehead against the window casement.

Yes, she was fatigued beyond words. Weary of always looking over her shoulder, wondering who might betray them next. Fearing that she would grow careless and endanger their lives. Worrying that Chris would slip and forget what name he was going by at present or reveal his true identity. Or fall. Or become ill and require medical attention she could ill afford.

How long could she continue living like this?

Squaring her shoulders and jutting her chin upward, she tightened her jaw. *For as long as it takes, Sarah Elizabeth Martha Paine.* Santano would pay for his treachery—someday.

Perchance... just perchance Gregor McTavish with his connections to Stapleton Shipping and Supplies could help in that regard, too. For Santano captained a stolen ship.

And she possessed the documentation to prove it.

Four

Gregor lounged against the wall outside the barrel-maker's shop. Pretending preoccupation in the cuff of his coat sleeve, he examined the many barrels from the corner of his eye. Passersby wouldn't notice anything out of the ordinary. Just another London dandy more concerned with his attire than the hardworking people nearby.

Och, nae one with eyes in their head would mistake my hulkin' form for a prissy cove.

His practiced eye detected no sign of the lad.

Was he here, hidden in a barrel?

Crouched behind one?

Had he left?

Och, Gregor hoped not.

What would he tell Sydney?

Switching his attention to the bustling wharf, he searched for Santano's compatriots. Satisfied none loitered nearby, he adjusted his hat to partially shade his face.

How he loathed playing the part of a conceited fop. He hadn't a doubt, given his size, he looked utterly ridiculous.

"Kipp, laddie, yer sister sent me to fetch ye. Ye dinna ken

me, and ye've nae reason to trust me." Not so much as a rustle met his quiet words. "Sydney said to tell ye that Satan has found ye, and ye're to come with me."

He nodded as two naval officers strode past, their cheerful blue uniforms neat and pristine.

The lid of the fourth barrel down shifted. Hazel eyes almost the exact shade as his sister's peeked between a one-inch gap.

Gregor gave the minutest inclination of his head to let the lad know he'd seen him. "She's safe and waitin' for us. She's verra worried about ye, though."

Another swift survey of the docks eased his mind, and straightening, he motioned to the driver of a wagon laden with bags of grain and covered by a tarp. He and McGarry already had arranged a place between the grain sacks for Kipp to hide.

"Kipp, stay where ye are until yonder wagon parks in front of the barrels." Recalling what his sister had said about him, Gregor gave simple directions. "Ye need to crawl inside. There's a place prepared for ye. Be careful ye aren't seen. McGarry here is my friend. He'll take ye to my warehouse. That's where yer sister is."

The lid settled into place once more, and satisfied that the lad understood, Gregor crossed to meet McGarry.

With a click of his tongue, McGarry drove the wagon across the dock and positioned it at an angle, so the rear faced the barrels. He climbed down from the driver's seat and, after yanking the tarp halfway up the wagon bed, clasped Gregor's hand before moving to rest against the freight wagon's far side.

One knee cocked, he jabbed a thumb toward the wagon load and wiped his brow with the back of his other hand. "Thirty sacks of oats for yer laird."

Ewan had no more need for oats than Gregor required bells on his boots. Nevertheless, he nodded and patted the horse's wither. The animal nickered softly and shifted his feet.

He rubbed between the horse's ears. "Dinna be too hasty delivering them, McGarry. I'm takin' my time returnin' to the office, in case I'm bein' watched. Wait for me at the rear of the warehouse."

Gregor turned and slapped his palm atop a grain sack. He nodded once more as if satisfied with his purchase and shook McGarry's hand. Rounding the wagon, he caught the boy's eye. "Stay down, ye ken?"

Face pale and his gaze wary, the lad acknowledged the request with a slight shifting of his frightened eyes.

"Och, there's a good lad."

With a casual wave, Gregor pulled his collar higher against the wind as he sauntered off. He took his time returning to his offices, stopping to chat with several acquaintances along the way. The whole while, he kept guarded and alert, watching for any indication he was followed.

At the Seven Seas, he ordered a warm, dark ale and sipped it slowly, probing every nook and cranny he could see for Santano and his men. Their absence likely meant they still searched for the Blanes.

As he strolled back to his lodgings, he pondered his impulse to help Sydney. In general, he wasn't a man given to indulging whims, much less rescuing damsels in distress. *Och, but this lass has sunshine in her hair and berries on her lips. And her eyes. Those eyes. Even a kelpie could drown in their beautiful pools.*

On the other hand, lowlife bullies like Santano and his cronies irritated Gregor. He flexed his gloved hands. Too many months of sitting at a desk and not enough riding, tramping through the Highlands, hunting, training, or some other sort of physical exertion at Craiglocky had him restless and itching for a good grapple.

How much longer would he procrastinate and delay the

inevitable return to Scotland? A wee bit longer, it seemed, as he'd decided to help a lass and her brother.

If Sydney were to be believed, the rumors circulating about how Santano acquired the *Mary Elizabeth* were true. He wasn't the first ship's captain to tread the thin line between lawlessness and honest ventures.

At this moment, Gregor could point out half a dozen ships gently rocking in the Thames's waters, engaging in one form of questionable commerce or another. Privateering might be outlawed, but he, as well as everyone else who worked the docks, knew smuggling and raids continued.

Likely, Santano possessed forged documents giving him ownership of the vessel.

Stapleton's warehouse came into view, and a slight movement drew his attention to the upper story windows.

Sydney watched, and by thunder, she bloody well needed to take more care not to be seen.

Removing his hat, he looked overhead, squinting as if he examined the petulant sky then cast a casual glance about him, hoping to God no one else had noticed her.

Gregor hadn't quite decided what he was going to do with her and her brother, but once he'd determined to aid someone, he didn't turn his back on them. If any two people required help, it was the Blanes.

That a bonnie lassie such as she managed to keep from being forced into prostitution or being set upon by the riffraff infesting London's docks, was a testament to her keen intellect and cunning.

Hopefully, he hadn't been an unsuspecting victim of both.

He unlocked the office door, and after stepping inside, slid the bolt home once more. He had yet to divest his outerwear before footsteps thumped upon the risers.

"Where is my brother?"

"Lass, stay out of sight."

"I sent you to fetch Chris, Highlander. Where. Is. He?" Panic riddled her voice.

"Dinna fash yerself. A friend of mine has the lad hidden in a wagon filled with bags of oats. They should be at warehouse doors, even now."

After removing his coat and hat, then draping his gloves across another curved arm of the porcelain-tipped oak coat rack beside the door, he wandered in front of the window so that anybody observing the establishment wouldn't suspect anything.

He stretched, flexing his spine and yawned. Selecting a ledger from his desk, he nonchalantly glanced at the window. Nothing. Flipping the journal open, he casually ambled toward the rear of the building.

"Was he all right?" she asked, only a hint of her earlier alarm evident in her voice.

Upon reflecting briefly, he said, "Aye, I think so. He looked well enough. A wee bit scared, but that's to be expected. I'm goin' to let yer brother inside. Remain out of sight and wait for the lad upstairs. We'll decide what to do with the two of ye while he's eatin'."

CHRIS GOBBLED the simple fare Gregor prepared. A piece of bread in one hand and a chicken leg in the other, his mouth bulging, he chomped away.

"Slow down. You're going to choke," Sarah fondly admonished.

Chris turned a boyish grin on her and, dropping the chicken, accepted the cup of water she offered.

"Lass, I need to speak with ye." *In private*, Gregor mouthed.

She squinted slightly at him, but his striking face and keen gaze gave nothing away. Fine lines creased the corners of his eyes, suggesting he was a man given often to mirth. "All right, Mr. McTavish." Patting Chris's shoulder, she gently reprimanded, "Slow down, darling. There's plenty of food."

For a change.

Taking a bite of cheese, Chris nodded and continued to inhale the fare.

As she followed Gregor into the sitting room, she shivered and brushed her hands up and down her arms before taking a seat in one of the oversized chairs. At once, the cat began rubbing himself against her legs.

Gregor knelt before the hearth, and after adding coal to the grate and lighting it, replaced the fender. She hadn't even had a fireplace or a stove in the one-room hovel they'd called home. Many a night, she'd wrapped Chris in her arms, holding him tight to still his quaking. And hers, too.

That first winter had been the godawful worst. Accustomed to much warmer temperatures, even with hats, gloves, coats, and wrapped in two blankets, her very bones had ached with cold.

Cat continued to make little chirping noises and nudged her ankles.

"Come here." She gathered the tubby feline into her arms, burying her face in his fur.

Cat closed his eyes, and contented rumbles echoed from his fluffy chest.

"I've never had a pet, except for Biscuit, my yellow-billed parrot. I always wanted a dog, though. Once, when I was a little girl, I saw a long, skinny dog with short legs at Port Royal. He was black with reddish-brown markings and looked like a long sausage with fat feet. He was the most adorable thing I've ever seen. If I ever have a dog, I want one like that," she declared with a firm nod.

Not much chance of that ever happening.

Not when she could scarcely feed herself and Chris.

Cutting Gregor a side-eyed peek through her lashes, mischievousness swept her. "And I shall name it Sausage."

The latter, she declared to make the Highlander laugh and see if she'd been right about the lines framing his eyes.

He sliced her a disbelieving look and chuckled, the sound a mellow rustle deep in his chest, as he settled into the other chair.

She hid a grin in Cat's back. *Very nice indeed.* She quite liked his laugh.

Some men's were harsh and grating, but his reverberated in his chest, a welcoming, warm invitation to join in his humor. Sarah also liked his melodious brogue. It, too, invited one to listen to his lilting speech. To snuggle into his chest, place her ear upon the vast expanse, and melt into the sound.

"Biscuit? Ye named a bird *Biscuit*?" He slapped his knee and chortled again. "And ye want to name a dog Sausage?"

The bird's name wasn't *that* funny.

She raised an eyebrow. Her most reproachful one. "Must I remind you that you have a fat feline named *Cat*, Highlander? And you dare laugh because, as a little girl, I couldn't pronounce hibiscus?" Another wave of melancholy bathed her. "I had to leave her behind. I don't know what happened to her."

He'd removed his coat and rolled up his shirt sleeves. Resting his forearms on his knees, sympathy softened his face. "I am sorry, lass. Ye've no' had an easy time of it, but we need to decide what to do next. I dinna think Santano will easily give up lookin' for ye."

The coals glowed reddish-orange, their flames radiating delicious heat. The high sides of the chair captured the warmth, and for the first time in a long while, Sarah enjoyed a toasty fire as well as a small sense of contentment.

Keeping her expression carefully neutral, she threaded her fingers in Cat's fur. He arched his back, a contented kitty smile upon his broad face.

"I know we do, Mr. McTavish, and I don't wish to impose upon you further—"

He lifted a wide palm, halting her. "It's too late for second thoughts. I willna abandon ye and yer brother now."

She hadn't even had to ask him. He'd volunteered of his own accord. It had been so long since anyone had cared about or helped her.

"But I do need to ken who ye really are." His tone changed the merest bit, and all signs of amusement fled his features. His blue-gray gaze probed hers, looking into the depths of her soul, and Sarah barely refrained from squirming.

Averting her attention, she swallowed twice. No one in England knew. Other than her grandmother and the viscountess's odious butler. "I concede you've no reason whatsoever to trust me," she said softly, still unwilling to take the final step and reveal her true identity.

Relaxing back in his chair, he hooked an ankle over his knee, totally at ease, watching her from beneath hooded eyes. "And ye've nae reason to trust me, either, but we're beyond that, dinna ye think?" The palms of both hands splayed open, his voice held no censure.

She acknowledged the truth of his words and lifted her chin a couple of inches, although her attention remained on the flames frolicking behind the grate.

"Let's begin again, shall we, lass?" He pressed a massive arm to his chest and dipped his chin in a mock semblance of a bow.

Eyebrows scrunched, she angled her head. What the devil was he about?

"I am Gregor Lieth Conall McTavish of Craiglocky Keep, cousin to the Laird Ewan McTavish, who is also Viscount

Sethwick. His wife, Yvette, owns Stapleton Shipping and Supplies, and just under a year ago, I left the Highlands to manage these London offices. I have a twin, Alasdair, and my parents Duncan and Kitta live at Craiglocky too."

He clasped a hand across his abdomen, drawing her reluctant attention to his muscled forearms once more. This was no weak fop. From his broad shoulders straining the fabric of his shirt, and the well-muscled thighs defined by his fawn-colored trousers, the Highlander was a fabulous specimen of masculine power and grace.

"Now, tell me who ye are." He rested his square chin with the merest hint of golden stubble on his fist. "And I'll have the truth this time, *Sassenach*."

FIVE

"*S* *assenach*?" Sarah tried the odd word on her tongue. "What does it mean?"

"Saxon and dinna try to change the subject."

She shouldn't be surprised he'd uncovered her secret. Continuing to withhold her identity was moot at this juncture. Particularly if he agreed to deliver a letter to Lady Rolandson on her behalf.

Burying her fingers in Cat's fur, she scanned his living quarters for the umpteenth time. More for a reason to stall than any lingering curiosity about his living quarters. How had she missed the massive sword propped in the corner by the door? Surely the monstrous thing was impossible to wield.

"Lass...?"

His persistence struck a discordant nerve, but Gregor was right. Santano had spies everywhere, and logic decreed it was only a matter of time before he found her and Chris if they remained in London. But to put her faith in this man she'd only known a couple of hours...

She must.

He'd kept his promise to bring Chris to her safely, surely that meant something.

Filling her lungs with air, she made her decision. "I'm Sarah Paine, and my brother is Christopher. My father was Captain Aaron Paine of the *Mary Elizabeth*. My mother Mary is—*was she still alive?*—was the only child of...aristocrats."

Anger surged through her toward her callous grandmother and the fiend responsible for her father's death. She squeezed her fists tight, her nails biting into her palms and forming crescents before forging onward.

"Santano and other miscreants commandeered my father's ship, killing everyone aboard who refused to join in their mutiny. Chris and I fled Jamaica, but our mother was too ill to travel. We've been hiding in London since under assumed identities. I fear Santano pillaged our home, as well." Bitter tears burned her eyes as she wrestled to control her emotions.

Moments like these, when Sarah let her thoughts stray to Mama, and wondering if she yet lived, were almost unbearable. The not knowing gnawed at her peace of mind. And the guilt she carried. That was nearly as awful.

Every day, she wished she'd insisted Mama leave, too. Then her wiser self would argue; her mother wouldn't have survived the ocean voyage, and she'd known that. Not ill and recovering from a fever as she had been.

Sarah shifted, the weight of the hidden pocket pressing into her thigh. McTavish didn't need to know about the key or chest. Not yet, if ever. He'd already endangered his life by helping them. "As I said, Mr. McTavish, I don't wish to impose, but you are correct. It's far too late for that, I fear."

"And ye've nae relatives or friends who might take ye in?" His chin between his thumb and pointer finger, his astute gaze probed her, looking into her very soul.

A droll smile twisted Sarah's mouth. "My maternal grandmother refused to see Chris and me when we arrived in

London. We were turned away at the door and ordered to never return."

Eyebrows pulled tight at the inner corners, Gregor scratched his jaw, his expression thoughtful. "Is it possible she didna ken ye'd called?"

"I suppose it is, but don't servants take orders from their employers? The butler vowed most emphatically that she wasn't at home to *us*. I'm sure you know that often means the homeowner may very well be peeking at their unwanted visitors from behind the draperies."

He acknowledged the truth of her words with a slight shifting of his eyes, more blue than gray at the moment. It must be his sky-blue double-breasted waistcoat that caused the color to change. "Who is yer grandmother?"

"The Viscountess Rolandson. Have you heard of her?"

Surprise well-seasoned with reservation flickered across Gregor's face. His reaction reconfirmed Sarah's own impression of her grandmother.

"Aye, though I've never met her personally." He rubbed one finger alongside his nose. "She has a reputation for bein'… starchy."

A polite way of saying she was a crotchety, unforgiving, demanding, grudge-holding old tabby. Not likely she'd be any more eager to meet her daughter's children now than she had been three years ago.

Changing the subject to a more immediate need, she said, "I'm not sure how Santano's men found us, but I'm positive our room has been searched." Ransacked. Their few possessions destroyed.

"So ye've nae place to go then, Miss Paine?"

She chuckled and swiped her stiff hair off her shoulder. "Don't you think it's a little late for formalities, Highlander? Please call me Sarah, and no, at the moment, Chris and I are without accommodations." Such a polite way of saying they were homeless.

"I'll only call ye by yer given name if ye do the same with me," he said.

She agreed with a brief inclination of her head

He gave a short, decisive nod, as well. "Ye can stay with me for now. I ken it's no' at all proper, but I think it's the safest course. I have an extra chamber." Gregor angled a pickle-sized thumb to the doorway beside the kitchen. "As long as nae one kens ye are here, yer reputation shouldna suffer."

She laughed again, this time genuinely amused. Nearly five and twenty, she'd long since given up on society's strictures.

Not that she'd ever really followed them. Life in Jamaica was much different, much more relaxed and forgiving than stodgy England. Mama had seen that Sarah could conduct herself with poise and decorum in the stuffiest English drawing rooms, but given a choice, she'd prefer to be barefoot and bonnetless.

"I assure you, Gregor, I've stopped fretting about my reputation. In the past three years, Chris and I have lived in tenements where prostitutes entertained their patrons in the room next door. You know as well as I do, my repute is beyond salvaging."

An inarticulate sound of denial reverberated in his throat, but the truth rested in his honest gaze.

She lifted her shoulders, and Cat shot her a why-are-you-disturbing-my-sleep-by-moving-look. "I'm not feeling sorry for myself because I'll manage somehow. But I do worry about Chris."

"As I said, lass, ye can stay here for now. Yer brother can sleep on the couch, and ye can take the bedroom. It locks from within." That almost seemed an afterthought to reassure her. He drummed his fingers, the nails square and clean, upon his broad knee. "I'm goin' to send letters 'round to friends and relatives and recruit a wee bit of help on yer behalf."

She crossed her ankles, very conscious of her holey socks and her breech's soiled, ragged edges. A long soak in the tub would be heaven. And a cup of steaming tea, liberally laced with milk and sugar.

Oh, my that sounds wonderful.

She scrunched her nose. "I thought all of your relatives lived in Scotland."

It was Gregor's turn to chuckle, that contagious rumble that called to her, and she couldn't help but smile in return. He scratched his temple, still grinning. "Och, only partially true. I'm either related by marriage or acquainted with a goodly number of peers who live in London or have residences within a day's ride."

Chris wandered in from the kitchen and made straight for the couch. Bluish shadows framed his eyes, a testament that he'd not been sleeping well, either. Lying on his side, one hand nestled beneath his hollow cheek, his eyelids drifted closed.

She stood and crossed to her brother. After placing a throw pillow beneath his head, she brushed his hair off his brow. "Poor thing. He's exhausted."

"Na more than ye, I'd wager." Gregor rubbed his nape before saying, "I also advise ye to write yer grandmother and tell her what has transpired. Unless she's completely without a heart, she'll nae turn away her grandchildren."

Sarah wasn't positive that the viscountess had ever possessed a heart, and any organ in the woman's chest had long since turned to stone.

He considered Chris then rose and disappeared into one of the bed chambers for a moment. When he returned, he carried a blanket, which he tenderly laid across the already fast asleep child.

An unfamiliar sensation uncurled in Sarah's chest.

A perilous thing for a woman relying on her wits and independence to survive. She had no room for emotional entanglements. But this burly, attractive Highlander was proving to be the most kind, considerate man she'd ever met. The type of decent, honorable man a woman could fall in love with.

A woman not afraid for her life and responsible for a crippled child. A woman so accustomed to leeriness and mistrust, to living in a constant state of fear, she'd forgotten the happy, carefree woman she'd once been.

He ran his practiced gaze over her shoddy garments. "We also need to see ye attired in clothin' befittin' a viscountess's granddaughter. All the more reason I've decided to seek help from my female family and friends."

"I haven't the funds to spare to purchase clothing for myself or Chris." She refused to be embarrassed by that fact. She'd done well by her brother, keeping them fed, not always full, but they hadn't starved. She'd also kept a roof over their heads and managed to do so without compromising her virtue.

"Dinna worry about the funds. I'd offer to pay for them, but I can see by the independent spark in yer eye, ye'd refuse me and tell me to bugger myself, to boot."

"Right you are, Highlander." The small upward tick of her lips contradicted her rejoinder. She enjoyed bantering with him. Much more than she ought.

"Between Ewan's sisters and our friends, I've nae doubt they can spare everythin' ye need from the skin out," he said.

She couldn't prevent the blush scorching her cheeks at the mention of undergarments. Men simply didn't discuss something so intimate, but he continued on as if he hadn't crossed the mark or noticed her discomfiture.

"They'll be happy to do it too." He rolled his eyes. "Nothin' those noble ladies delight in more than a waif or an orphan to take under their protection."

"I hardly qualify as, either," she retorted, her tone drier than flour.

Did he genuinely expect her to accept charity from women she didn't know? Her pride chafed mightily at the idea, but dash it to ribbons, he was right. Making a positive impression the first time she met her grandmother and entered Polite Society was imperative.

"By the way, Sarah, I saw ye peekin' from the window when I returned." He tempered his rebuke with a rakish smile. "Ye must be more careful."

Damn. She'd thought she'd been so cautious.

"Remind Chris to stay away from the windows too," he advised, turning to examine the long panels. "In fact, until we're sure that Santano is convinced yer no' here, let's leave the curtains drawn."

He crossed to the windows and released the tiebacks on either side. With a whoosh and a rustle, the crimson velvet floated across the glass, obstructing the view.

Wouldn't that alert Santano or his thugs if they still watched the building?

"If ye're wonderin' if that'll make Santano's bounders suspicious, it willna. I generally leave the draperies closed. I'm unused to neighbors and like my privacy," he said by way of an explanation. "My housekeeper opens them the days she cleans."

He'd read her mind—unnerving and disquieting. Exciting, too.

"I intend to order a couple of warehouse workers to be extra vigilant and patrol the premises, just in case Santano or his men return. In the meanwhile, pen a letter to yer grandmother, and I'll make sure it's delivered."

He'd thought this through, hadn't he? But how long could she and Chris realistically stay here?

"However, there is one small kink in my plan, lass."

And here it came. The "but" she'd been anticipating.

"I'm sure ye noticed the other desk in the office," he said.

Sarah nodded, absently rubbing her hands up and down her arms. She had but had been too distraught to puzzle over it. "Yes, I thought it a bit odd that no one else worked in the office of an establishment this large."

"I do have a clerk, but he's been ill the past three days. I dinna want Baker to ken ye're here, so I'll have to contrive an excuse to keep him away." Gregor squatted before the fire and added more coal.

Convinced he did so on her account, another spark of gratitude fluttered in Sarah's chest.

Hearth broom in hand, he glanced over his shoulder. "As I mentioned, I have a woman who cleans twice a week, on Tuesdays and Fridays."

He swept a smattering of coal dust into a small dust bin and dumped it into the fire. Once he'd replaced the tools, he began pacing the room, one hand on his nape, and the other on his lean hip.

"I think I must decline your kind offer." Though what she would do instead, she couldn't fathom. It made her head hurt to contemplate. Made the knot in her stomach tangle impossibly tighter. Sarah pressed her fingers between her eyes. "At the very least, your clerk will be curious, and your housekeeper mustn't see us here. It would be no small task to keep Chris quiet in any event."

Gregor might have confidence in them, but Santano wasn't above trickery, bribery, or other devilment to gain information. His man, Yeates, hadn't believed the Highlander.

She was sure of it.

"Nae so fast, lass. Mrs. Smith winna come for a couple of days, and I'm hopeful I shall either have ye settled with yer grandmother or one of my friends by then."

Neither idea appealed overly much, truth to tell. They were strangers, after all.

"As for Baker, he's a trustworthy sort. He'd nae betray ye. Still, I dinna want him here." He snapped his fingers, and a grin lit his eyes. "I have it. I'll send him to Scotland with the letter to my cousin. I'll also have him deliver my other missives. It winna be the first time I've done so, and he'll have nae reason to believe anythin' out of the ordinary is goin' on."

"Gregor, you ought to be aware that you're putting your life in danger by continuing to help us." She slid a swift look to Chris, assuring herself he slept on. He'd never been able to grasp the peril they faced. "Santano killed my father, and he may have my mother, as well. I don't doubt that he wouldn't hesitate to murder you, too."

He slipped a wicked-looking knife from his boot, holding it up for her to see. "Och, never fear, lass. I can defend myself and ye if need be. I never go anywhere without this." He pointed to the massive blade she'd spied earlier. "And trust me when I tell ye, I've some skill wieldin' a sword."

He didn't boast, merely stated a fact.

"I have a feeling, Gregor McTavish, you're skilled in a great many things." Of its own volition, her gaze strayed to his mouth. Lord help her and the naughty path her thoughts dared to trundle down.

At that moment, Cat stretched and opened his eyes, giving her such an astute look followed by a feline smile, and she swore the beast knew precisely what she was thinking. She hadn't yet admitted to herself, but something far more than gratitude to the Highlander held her in thrall.

Six

Awareness of Sarah as a desirable woman assailed Gregor as she stared at his lips. When her small tongue darted out and moistened the corner of her mouth, he almost groaned aloud. He'd been without a woman since leaving Scotland.

The cold English misses held little appeal for him. Until this frail tropical flower had burst headlong into his life.

His mouth dried, his nostrils flared, and wild Highland ponies galloped through his middle. Not since Lily—*nae, not even then*—had a woman piqued his interest as acutely. Dressed in the first stare of fashion, her shimmering flaxen hair twisted into an elaborate coiffure, a little flesh softening the sharp angles of her bones, and Sarah Paine would turn many a man's eye.

Who was he fooling? She'd snared his attention dressed like a beggar and scared senseless. Keen of wit, unselfish, valiant as any warrior, and lovely of face and figure, a man wouldn't soon forget her.

His gut tightened sickeningly.

Another reason to save her from Santano and the cretins

49

working for him. Gregor had no doubt they'd ravish her before slitting her throat.

He scratched an eyebrow, noting Cat now lay splayed like an arrogant Egyptian Sphinx atop Chris as the lad slept. Traitorous beast.

Sarah's safety wasn't the only thing compelling him to ask her to stay. She intrigued him as no other ever had, and he hoped to know her better away from the constraints of society and family. When she trotted off to her grandmother's—as he genuinely hoped she'd be able to—he wouldn't likely have the opportunity.

He was no fool.

Granddaughters to viscountesses didn't associate with those smelling of the shop. Though his cousin Ewan might hold dual titles, one an English viscountcy himself, more commonly than not, the *ton*'s denizens looked down their aristocratic noses at Scots.

Certainly, he was welcomed in the drawing rooms and gatherings of friends and family, but he seldom ventured into social circles beyond those. Neither highborn nor wealthy, he lacked two of the criteria that opened elitist *ton* doors.

If Lady Rolandson opted to recognize her grandchildren by inviting Sarah and Chris into her home, chances were, his association with Sarah would end. And he didn't want that to happen.

Not until he figured out why she fascinated him so, and he needed time to do that. With a silent sigh and single-minded purpose, he shoved his personal interest into a corner of his mind to be taken out and studied later at his leisure.

For now, although he'd known the lass mere hours, his foremost concern was keeping her hidden from Santano. He cleared his throat and scraped a hand through his hair. "I have a hip bath in the storage closet if ye'd like to heat water. Ye'll find linens and all else ye need there, as well."

Such thankfulness swept her face, one would think he might've offered her a palace. She clasped her hands and rocked back on her heels. "Oh, that sounds lovely." She plucked at her shabby shirt, scrunching her nose in an engaging manner. "But, I'm loath to put on my soiled clothes again."

"Aye." He allowed himself an extended perusal of her form. His scrutiny only intensified his attraction. "Mine are too big for ye. For the lad too." Gregor skewed his mouth sideways. He couldn't risk purchasing clothing for a child or a woman.

"It's of no matter." She combed her fingers through her long locks. "A bath will still be much appreciated."

"Wait." He snapped his fingers again. "Yvette collects clothin' for the poor. There's a barrel in the warehouse that's meant for Craiglocky with the next load of supplies. I'm sure I can locate somethin' for ye in there."

Mayhap even a bar of perfumed soap in the supplies intended for home, too.

He was positive Yvette wouldn't object if he confiscated a few of her personal toiletries. She could always order more, and as generous as she was, she wouldn't begrudge Sarah a cake of scented French soap.

"Prepare yer bathwater, and I'll see what I can pillage for ye to wear. Ye'll find a big pot in the storeroom to heat the water."

Shoes and undergarments might be an issue, but surely there was a discarded gown that would suit. It might not be the first stare of fashion, but given Sarah wore loose-fitting rags, he didn't think she'd complain.

At least until the ladies, he intended to write swept in to rescue her. They'd soon have her decked head to toe in Almack patroness-approved attire.

"Gregor?"

He turned back from the door. "Aye, lass?"

Indecision flickered in her eyes before she drew her shoulders back and marched across the floor. "I cannot thank you enough for what you've done for Chris and me. I vow, someday, somehow, I shall make it up to you."

Such sincerity rang in her voice, he couldn't help but admire her gumption.

His gaze dropped to the rosy, plump lower lip she'd been torturing for the past half an hour. Likely, she wasn't even aware she chewed the tender flesh when nervous or upset. What he'd like to do above all else was ask for a kiss.

Except, only the lowest cur bargained with a woman as desperate as her.

Still...

Slipping a handful of her hair over her shoulder, he gave her a naughty wink. "I can think of all sorts of creative ways ye might do that, my tropical flower, but I'll settle for a wee kiss from yer sweet mouth."

He couldn't resist seeing her reaction. As he suspected, she wasn't immune to him, either.

Her eyes rounded, filling with wonder, and her jaw slackened.

"I was but teasin' ye, lass." He gently pushed her mouth closed. "What kind of a blackguard do ye take me for?"

"Not a blackguard at all. You're a kind, decent, brave man." She thrust her hand out at him, and it was his turn to be taken aback. "I agree to your request."

No one need tell him a stupid ear-to-ear grin split his face. "Ye do?" He wrapped her small, rough hand in his and shook it.

"I do. But I choose when and where." She shoved his torso with her other palm. "Now find me suitable clothing, please. I cannot wait to bathe and wash my hair."

As Gregor thumped down the stairs, the vision of her

naked and dripping wet sifted into his imagination, and he missed the next step, nearly tumbling head over arse. Good thing it was the second to the last stair, or he might've broken his neck. "*Gude*, what's come over me?"

❧

ANOTHER TWO DAYS PASSED UNEVENTFULLY, and Sarah stirred the porridge as she listened for sounds that Gregor or Chris had awoken. Humming, she browned the sausages then checked the steeping tea.

Wearing a stained apron over the simple plaid morning dress he'd procured for her, she'd cooked meals and performed other small tasks, trying in some modest way to repay Gregor's kindnesses. And to keep her mind off the irrefutable fact that her grandmother didn't want to see her or Chris.

Her letter, delivered by Gregor himself to the butler—possessed with a face homelier than an old mule's back end, according to the Highlander—had gone unanswered.

Again.

What would she have done if Gregor had turned out to be a scoundrel?

Sarah dismissed the unnerving thought.

No sense fretting about something that hadn't come to pass, and she was quite confident at this juncture, wouldn't. That much she'd learned about him. Gregor McTavish was a man of honor.

Likewise, he awaited responses to the notes he'd sent, so she'd spent the past two days mending his clothing, tidying his already neat apartment, cooking, and reading from the pleasant and abundant assortment of books lining the shelves beside the window.

It had been so long since she relaxed and enjoyed a book, she felt wicked and indulgent.

Chris had been harder to keep amused.

He could barely read and grew bored quickly. Cat kept him entertained part of the time, but Chris had become increasingly restless. After Gregor's daily outing yesterday to seek word about Santano's whereabouts, he had returned with a few toys.

With Christmastide just over three weeks away, it wasn't surprising he'd easily found trinkets for Chris's amusement. Not only were shop windows full of tempting displays, but street vendors also hawked their handmade wares.

At first, she'd fretted someone might've seen him, but he'd assured her he'd been discreet. A wagoner made the purchases and delivered them to Stapleton's warehouse, concealed in a freight wagon of supplies.

Although she hated being further indebted to Gregor, the joy on Chris's face as he'd sat upon the floor, opening the packages had reminded her very much of the Yuletides celebrated in Jamaica, and Sarah couldn't refuse the well-intended gifts.

She hadn't observed Christmastide while in London. Pauper poor and barely able to keep themselves fed, so pinch-penny was she with money that gifts had been out of the question. She blamed Santano for that, too.

On his shopping sojourns, Gregor had obtained useful information.

The good news was the *Mary Elizabeth* was scheduled to sail in just over a week. Chances were, Santano wouldn't make port again for six months or more. The bad news was that it would make him much more desperate to find her and the key before he put out to sea.

She'd avoided the blackguard for three years. Surely with Gregor's help, she could manage another ten days. That gave her time to hatch a plan and leave London.

She couldn't argue that she found the Highlander

deucedly attractive, and his appeal increased with each passing day. Larger than the men she was accustomed to, his ruggedly handsome face and hands bore evidence of time spent in the sun. He wore his hair—as light as hers, though more honey-toned than flaxen—unfashionably long and tied back in a queue.

Few men in the Caribbean had passed Papa's scrutiny or had been permitted to call upon her. Truth to tell, no more than she could count on one hand, and none sparked more than a passing glance and a polite smile. Since arriving in London, romantic entanglements had been the last thing on her mind.

No, survival had been at the forefront of her thoughts for three years. For the first time since disembarking that fateful afternoon, she wasn't in a constant state of fear.

She owed Gregor McTavish much more than a promised kiss.

Touching the braid hanging over her right shoulder, she fingered the black ribbon.

He permitted her to borrow one of his, not wanting to raise questions by buying pins for her, although he might've asked one of his employees to do that, as well. Except he told the worker who'd bought the toys for him that they were gifts for his kin. His claim rang true since Yuletide, though no longer illegal, was still strongly discouraged by the Scottish Kirk.

It seemed he'd thought of everything, continually weighing the situation and the repercussions.

None of Santano's thugs had returned to the shop, but in case they did, the door to his living quarters remained locked at all times, and as Gregor had asked, she and Chris stayed away from the windows.

Sarah speared the drapery-covered windows a darkling look.

She'd much prefer the natural light but would take no chances of discovery. She'd dared a peek outdoors this morning, and the sky lay heavy with a peculiar pinkish-gray cloud cover. As it had the past several mornings, a thick layer of frost and ice covered every surface.

Once again, appreciation swelled within her breast and tears in her eyes, as well. Homeless, how would she and Chris have survived this freezing cold? They wouldn't have.

"I kent I smelled sausage."

Sarah whipped her attention to the doorway, very much aware of the virile man a few feet away.

Hair damp, and attired only in his boots, buckskins, and white lawn shirt, Gregor dominated the entrance. Lord, he was a gorgeous specimen of manhood. Under other circumstances, she might've been tempted to explore a relationship with him.

If he noticed her fascination, his mien in no way betrayed it. He inhaled a deep breath, patting his tummy. "I'm famished."

"You're always starving, Gregor."

She ran another gaze over him and couldn't help but appreciate his well-muscled, masculine form.

His blue-gray eyes twinkled with mirth, and she vowed he knew exactly the wanton thoughts she entertained.

Heat swept upward from her middle to her neck then to her cheeks. To cover her embarrassment, she waved the spoon toward the table. "Sit down. The food's almost ready."

"Mrs. Smith is due this afternoon." He took a seat, dwarfing the sturdy chair. "I've decided ye and Chris should hide in the warehouse. I've already prepared a place for ye."

So that's why he was late for breakfast. "That's a good idea." She nodded as she poured his tea.

"I dinna want to do anythin' out of my normal routine to alert anyone that ye're here." He said by way of an explanation as he lifted his knife and fork. "I expect responses to the letters I sent verra soon, too."

As he tucked into his meal, Sarah once again tried to understand the enigmatic Highlander. Nothing seemed to shake his confidence. He remained optimistic and encouraging, still adamant her grandmother would come 'round.

A sad smile tipped her mouth, and she hid it behind the teacup raised to her lips. Too bad, his optimism wasn't contagious.

The office bell clanged below.

Alert, his features tense, Gregor jerked his head up and put his finger to his lips. "*Shh.*"

SEVEN

Swallowing her fear, Sarah nodded and hands shaking, placed the cup back in its saucer. It took her a moment to settle it soundly and stop its clattering. Something as simple as an unexpected bell ringing and panic bubbled to the surface.

"Lock the door after me." Gregor patted her shoulder, his huge hand burning through the gown's thin fabric. The gesture had no doubt meant to soothe, but every time he touched her, sensual sparks lit.

No sooner had she turned the key in the lock than a sleepy-eyed Chris shuffled from the bedroom, rumpled and disheveled.

"Morning, sister."

"Good morning, darling. Did you sleep well?"

Yawning behind his hand, he nodded and blinked groggily.

Rather than take the bedchamber and have Chris sleep on the sofa, Sarah had chosen to sleep on the floor at the foot of his bed.

For years, they'd shared the same uncomfortable mattresses, but she conceded, she appreciated not having his bony elbows in her ribs or being walloped during one of his bad dreams. Not only did he still have nightmares, but he also walked in his sleep. Though not likely, she couldn't take a chance of him wandering from Gregor's apartment.

After she spent the first night on the floor, a feather tick, a thick coverlet, and another pillow had appeared in the chamber for her use. She hadn't said a word, but Gregor had noticed.

That was another thing she admired about him; his attention to little details and his consideration for others. As if she needed something else to add to the growing list of things he'd done to impress her.

"Come along. Breakfast is ready." Wrapping an arm around Chris's shoulders, Sarah hugged him to her side and guided him toward the kitchen. While he ate, she meant to bundle her bedding into the storage closet to prevent the housekeeper from becoming suspicious.

Holding a brown spotted horse atop cherry-red wheels, his favorite of the playthings that Gregor had given him, he gave her a lopsided smile. "I like it here, sister." He gave her a toothy grin and rubbed his left eye with the palm of his other hand. "I like Gregor and Cat too."

Sorrow and desolation whirled together, tightening her chest. She swallowed, then cleared her throat before painting on a bright smile. "I do as well, darling, but I told you already, we cannot stay. It's not safe for Gregor or for us."

Well, not until the *Mary Elizabeth* set sail, in any event. Then she'd have a few months' reprieve. She fully intended to abscond to somewhere Santano would never find them.

A pout pulled Chris's usually cheerful mouth downward as he settled into the chair. Several strands of hair fell over his forehead, concealing his left eye. "Are we never going to have a home again, Sister? Will we ever see Mama again?"

I honestly don't know.

He knew about Papa, but not Mama. The truth of it was, she didn't know whether her mother still lived. A tiny spark of hope glimmered that she did.

Sarah couldn't tell him they mightn't ever have a home. Most likely wouldn't ever see their mother again, so she did what any loving sister would do and distracted him. "Have you named your pony yet?" She dipped her chin toward the toy horse he rolled back and forth before him.

"Yes. Brownie, 'cause he has brown spots." He pointed to the irregular circles.

"Most appropriate." If not entirely original.

Holding the toy up for her inspection, he broke into a wide grin. "Gregor promised to teach me to ride. I want to learn on a pony just like this."

Spooning porridge into his bowl, she glanced up. "He did? When was that?"

"While you bathed the other day." One of its wheels squeaking, he rolled the toy across the table again. "He showed me a big book with horse pictures. His cousin raises them."

Botheration. Gregor shouldn't be making promises of that nature. Chris didn't understand that sometimes people said things to be kind: things they didn't intend to or simply couldn't do.

The key rattled in the outer door lock, and she raised a finger to her lips as she swiftly closed the kitchen door before placing Chris's food on the table. The unmistakable sound of the bolt sliding home reassured her, and she released the breath burning her lungs.

A moment later, Gregor swaggered in looking entirely too cocky and pleased with himself. "It's all right, lass, lad. Just a messenger, droppin' off an order for me. Truth to tell, I didnae expect him until later this mornin'."

She poured Gregor fresh tea before retaking her seat. Never had she known a man to drink more tea than Gregor

McTavish, and he drank his brew sweet. Three lumps of sugar per cup.

Papa had preferred black coffee.

Grinning, as if he were Saint Nick himself, Gregor strode to the table, holding two large brown paper-wrapped bundles. "I have a surprise for ye."

My, the man did enjoy giving to others. She'd never known anyone with as generous a nature.

Chomping on a bite of sausage, Chris grinned. "What is it?"

"Chris, chew your food first, then talk," Sarah gently admonished him. She turned the same starchy eye upon Gregor. "What have you done? I told you, I don't feel right accepting anything else from you. Besides, won't those raise suspicions?" She wiggled her fingers at the packages.

If anything, Gregor's grin grew bigger, pure delight sparking in his eyes.

She pressed a hand to her frolicking belly. *Gads*, when he smiled at her like that, it took all of her will to cobble together a coherent thought.

"Alas, that's the beauty of it." He gave a mischievous wink and patted Chris's shoulder. "I used the Yuletide as an excuse. I dinna ken why I didna think of it before. Dafty of me, really. I had a half dozen more packages wrapped and delivered to the kirk for the poor, so nae one kens the truth."

"But, Gregor, the Scots don't celebrate Christmastide." Even she knew that.

Drawing himself up, he sliced Chris—busily eating and playing with his horse—a sideways glance. "Och, but I'm in England now. Would ye begrudge me the enjoyment of the tradition? I hear all sorts of savory foods and sweets are served." He patted his flat stomach.

Clever, endearing man.

"I ken there are kissin' boughs and mistletoe too."

Rocking back on his heels, he hugged the packages, causing the stiff paper to crackle in protest. His devilish wink made her blood sidle warmer still, and heat stung her cheeks. "Should a lucky gentleman catch a bonnie lassie beneath either, he's entitled to a wee kiss."

Lord. A kiss from a man like him would no doubt set her blood afire and singe her hair.

"You're taking advantage of the situation, Gregor McTavish." She attempted to sound stern, but her voice came out rather breathier than she'd intended. "Your breakfast grows cold. Why don't you set those aside? We can open them later."

"Aye, lass." He winked again, obviously pleased as Punch with himself and enjoying this misadventure far too much. Before she could think of a suitable retort, he disappeared into the main room, returning shortly with letters between his forefinger and thumb. "I forgot to tell ye. I've had responses from Countesses Ramsbury and Clarendon and the Duchess of Harcourt."

Her confusion must've shown on her face.

"The countesses are Ewan's sisters, and her grace is the wife of one of Ewan's closest chums," he explained as if it were the most common thing in the world to be on intimate terms with nobles.

"My, you do have lofty connections, don't you?" Sarah settled into her chair and, after draping the serviette across her lap, cocked her head.

"Aye. I do." Gregor shied his eyebrows high up his forehead and chuckled. "I'm still waitin' to hear from the Baroness de Deavaux-Rousset, the Countess of Luxmoore, the Viscountess Warrick, and Lady Sethwick."

Spoon midway to her mouth, Sarah gaped. "Oh, my stars. You weren't jesting about knowing a goodly number of peeresses. Have you imposed upon all of them on my behalf?"

She nearly groaned aloud from mortification. But if it benefited Chris, her damnable pride would have to suffer.

"Aye," he said, teacup in hand and not the least bit repentant. "And a few noblemen, too."

A humiliated groan did escape her then.

Two days ago, she'd believed he exaggerated. Knowing what she did about him now, she'd learned he was a man of his word. Having never spent any time in the company of aristocrats, the idea of doing so made her increasingly anxious.

Imposing upon Gregor was one thing, but asking favors from high-ranking *haut ton* denizens?

That was quite another, and she wasn't altogether sure she'd measure up.

He cut a piece of sausage then speared it with his fork. "They're all either relatives or friends of Ewan who've become family friends, as well."

"You're very close to your cousin, aren't you?"

Sarah hadn't any cousins.

Mama had been an only child, and Papa rarely spoke of his family. He'd run away to the sea as a young boy. Once, he'd mentioned his drunkard of a father's ham-like fists and the beatings he'd endured. She had no idea if any of his relatives lived, and considering what little she knew of them, she wasn't keen to find out.

Chewing, Gregor nodded.

"Aye. Even the Fergusons, my step-cousins, are as close as if they were my own flesh and blood." He aimed his fork toward the main room. "I want ye to see the surprise I have for ye." Impatient as a lad, he wiped his mouth. He stood and extended his hand.

Sarah stared at it for a moment.

Ever so slowly, she fit hers into his great paw. His calloused palm swallowed her hand in a warm, comforting grip. Her logical side cautioned against imprudence. The woman who was increasingly taken with Gregor ignored wisdom. Leaving the dishes for later, she permitted him to urge her and Chris to sit upon the sofa.

Immediately upon spying her, Cat hopped from the windowsill and sauntered over. Giving Gregor a disdainful look, he twitched his whiskers and jumped into her lap.

"I believe ye've replaced me in his affections." Pleasure rather than envy tinged his observation.

Feeling only slightly guilty, for she enjoyed having a pet around, Sarah scratched Cat's ears. At once, his rumbling purr filled the room.

Chris ran a hand down Cat's side. He proceeded to make horse sounds as he rolled his toy along the sofa's arm.

Gregor handed her a package, requiring her to move Cat to the side to lay it atop her thighs.

White whiskers twitching, he gave her a haughty look, his green-yellow eyes narrowed peevishly.

His face animated with anticipation, Chris fidgeted beside Sarah.

"Here ye are, lad." Gregor passed him the smaller of the two bundles. "Let me ken if ye need help with the string."

One more thing to raise Gregor in her estimation. He offered to assist Chris, but always encouraged her brother to try everything on his own.

After a bit of fumbling, Chris managed to untie the string. He flipped the package over and unfolded the paper. Eyes wide with delight, he lifted a hunter green tailcoat trimmed in black velvet. A charcoal, jade green, and silver-striped waistcoat complimented the coat and black pantaloons. Stockings, a shiny new pair of shoes, along with a pristine white cravat, and new underthings lay beneath the suit.

Her brother ran his fingers over the fabric, his expression awed. "For me?"

"Aye, laddie." Gregor gave him a tender smile and ruffled his hair.

Chris sniffed and swiped the moisture from his face with his forearm, and Sarah thought her heart would burst from gratitude.

"What do you say, Chris?"

His eyes glistening, he gave Gregor one of his winning sideways smiles. "Thank you, Gregor."

"Ye're welcome, son. Now should yer sister open hers?"

Chris gave an eager nod, his wavy hair brushing his ratty collar. His hair needed trimming. Perhaps later today, she'd ask Gregor if he had a pair of scissors she could borrow.

Feeling somewhat self-conscious, Sarah untied her package. She couldn't suppress the gasp of pleasure upon turning the brown paper back to reveal a stunning gold and crimson gown—by far the loveliest she'd ever seen. Beneath the gown lay matching slippers, gloves, stockings, a fan, chemise, and short stays.

A blush heated her cheeks that he'd selected something so intimate for her.

"Ye might need to make alterations." He flicked a big hand over the garments. "I guessed on yer sizes based on what ye're wearin' now."

She glanced down at the apron, covering her simple dress. The clothes he'd fetched from the donation barrel were every bit as appreciated as these lovely gifts, though in an entirely different way. It seemed his thoughtfulness knew no bounds.

As far as alterations went, Sarah possessed talent with a needle. "I've been remaking our clothes from cast-offs..." She faltered as humiliation brought a flush to her face. "What I mean to say is, I can easily manage any alterations required."

"I assumed as much." A smile bent his mouth, revealing the straight row of his teeth as something more than appreciation kindled in his eyes. "I haven't thanked ye for mendin' my clothes."

Delicious heat bathed her, and to hide her consternation, she ran her palm over the gown. "Gregor, this is lovely, just gorgeous." It truly was. "But wherever will I wear such a creation?" Her gaze questioning, she met Gregor's eyes. Pride and *affection?* shone there. She quailed to think about how much the garments had cost. A warehouse supervisor didn't earn wages enough to be able to afford luxurious clothes such as these.

Had someone else paid for them?

Who?

Looking entirely too self-satisfied, he joined her on the couch and bold as brass took her hand in his and squeezed it. "That, *jo,* is part of the surprise. Ye ken those letters?"

The ones he'd just shown her a few minutes ago? Had he read them already?

"Yes," she agreed cautiously, setting the bundle on her lap aside.

"The Duchess of Harcourt is hostin' a Christmastide soirée in just under three weeks, and yer grandmother is invited. Trust me, given the Harcourts' influence and social standin', the dowager viscountess will attend. Her grace will see to it."

Proud as a peacock, he was. She almost expected him to puff out his chest. A dance and musical? Sarah closed her eyes. Lord, help her.

"Gregor, you must know, I've never spent so much as a minute in the company of an aristocrat. I shall embarrass us all, to be sure."

"Och, no' a bit of it. Ye'll be fine. They are kind people, Sarah," he assured her soothingly.

Hmph. There were degrees of kindness, and a gauche usurper plodding about their elegant homes with no knowledge of which spoon or fork ought to be used for what, surely wouldn't endear them to her pitiful cause.

"I have no voice, nor can I play an instrument," she murmured, twisting her hands in her apron. How she hated this inferior feeling.

"I'll make sure ye aren't called upon to do, either."

But she would be expected to dance. A lady of refinement might be excused the former for lack of talent or opportunity, but dancing? No. She was doomed. She flopped back against the sofa. "Gregor, I don't know how to dance."

<h1 style="text-align:center">EIGHT</h1>

"Och, lass, I'll teach ye." Gregor grasped Sarah's hand, and before she could object, pulled her to her feet.

A blush tinted her cheeks, but she didn't resist his urging.

"Now what would ye like to learn first? A Scottish Reel? A cotillion?" He dropped his voice to a husky whisper. "The deliciously wicked waltz?"

Her pretty hazel eyes wide, she blinked up at him. "I honestly have no idea."

He most definitely preferred the waltz. It gave him an excuse to hold her in his arms, but wisdom decreed he take a slower pace. "Let's start with somethin' simple then. The Hole in the Wall, I think. No' too difficult, even if we do require another couple to do it properly." His attention shifted to Chris. "Would ye care to learn, laddie?"

"Och, nae." Chris's vehement denial, as well as his attempt at Scots, sent Sarah and Gregor into peals of mirth.

"It's to be just ye and me then." Gregor bent into a formal bow. "Madam."

Laughing, a bit self-consciously, she dipped into a less than graceful curtsy.

A wee frown pulled his eyebrows together.

Sarah had no experience with dancing or curtsying? Because there was no opportunity, or because her parents didn't participate in social functions? What he knew about Jamaica's societal hierarchy wouldn't fill a salt spoon.

Several minutes passed as he hummed and counted, teaching her the steps and movements. An adept pupil, she soon caught on. The intense concentration pursing her mouth and crinkling her eyes gave way to pleasure as they circled and crossed the floor.

"This is fun," she exclaimed as she stepped away with regal grace.

When was the last time she'd enjoyed herself? She hadn't done much of that these past few years, he suspected.

He chuckled to himself, drawing her attention.

A delicate golden eyebrow arched, and she skewed her mouth sideways. "Am I really so inept?"

"Nothin' of the sort, *jo*. I'm just imaginin' what my brother and cousins would say if they could see me givin' dance lessons." He, one of Craiglocky's fiercest warriors. He'd never hear the end of it.

"I think it the noblest of gestures." She made an elegant turn and passed him in the middle. "Although I must tell you, the idea of facing my grandmother when she's rejected every attempt to contact her sends a chill up my spine."

"Ye've nae need to fret, Sarah. For I am confident between all those ladies I mentioned and their husbands, we can contrive a solution to yer dilemma."

Her skeptical countenance suggested she wasn't so sure.

"I think ye've mastered this one. Let's try a quadrille, shall we? It's a wee bit more complicated." He held up a hand. "Take my hand." Sarah did so, and he said, "There are four couples for the set."

It was her turn to laugh. "I'm trying to picture you as a young man learning these steps. I'd be bound, at the time you'd rather have been climbing trees and such."

She had the right of it.

He'd often complained about learning the niceties required of Polite Society even in Scotland. Now though, as he swept an arm around her waist, leading her in a circle, he could kiss his mother for insisting he do so.

"Have ye ever given thought to visitin' Scotland?" His casual tone belied the question's importance.

What he truly wanted to know was if Sarah were offered a safe haven in the Highlands, would she go? And if she did, would he stay here in London? The Highlands had called to him more and more of late. His stint in London would soon come to an end. He could feel it in his pores. And if he and Sarah were both in Scotland...

Far too early to be harboring those types of musings.

Wasn't it?

Instead of answering, her gaze confused yet hopeful, she stared up at him. Her work-worn hand clasped in his, he was unable to break eye contact. As he searched her eyes, seeing himself reflected in the blue and gold flecks, he couldn't identify what transpired, but at that moment, his life changed forever.

I swear leannan, I'll do whatever is necessary to keep ye and yer brother safe.

To see them off London's streets and settled someplace comfortably, as well. Mayhap...explore this ever-growing fascination.

"Sister, can't we go for a walk. Please?" Chris pulled a face and gazed longingly toward the window.

Poor lad. He needed exercise and fresh air.

"I think that's enough dancing lessons for today." Sarah

withdrew her hand and stepped away, her eyes lowered. Caution had replaced her earlier enthusiasm.

She'd felt the connection too, and given the cool politesse that settled upon her, it frightened her. Sitting beside her brother, she fondly tussled his hair, several shades darker than hers. "No, darling, not right now. It's still not safe, and it's much too cold. Soon, though. I promise."

She glanced at Gregor for confirmation, and he hitched a shoulder, giving her an I'm-nae-sure-when-look. He'd be bound, given the pinkish glint to the sky, snow would soon cover London.

Had it snowed while she'd been in England other than a light blanketing?

He determined to take the boy's mind off his forced seclusion. "Tell me, lad. What's yer favorite part of Christmastide?"

Chris grinned, his face animated. "The food. Mama made gingerbread and plum pudding."

"I've never eaten, either," Gregor admitted. "Although, I'm fond of black bun and clootie dumplin', which I'm told is verra similar to plum puddin'."

"Black bun?" Sarah asked. "Is that a sort of bread?

"Nae, it's a fruitcake covered with pastry, usually served for Hogmanay." He closed his eyes, the image blooming behind his eyelids of the trestle table in Craiglocky's great hall sagging under the succulent feast.

"That's your New Year's celebration?"

"Aye."

"Gregor, you obviously miss Scotland a great deal." Sarah stood a couple of Chris's toy soldiers on their feet. "Why do you stay here?"

"A man likes to be in charge of his own destiny. I will never have that at Craiglocky." Yet, he contemplated returning. In a different role. Not cousin to the laird and son to Ewan's second-in-command.

He settled in one of the chairs before the fire, and after a moment, Sarah sank into the other and tucked her feet beneath her. "If you could do anything at all, Gregor, what would it be?" She probed his gaze, her interest genuine.

"Become a doctor, but it's too late at my age."

"No. It's not." She gave a vehement shake of her head. "If it's your passion, you should pursue it."

Rather than argue, he asked her the same question. "What about ye, lass?"

"If I had the means, I'd open a school for those less fortunate." She sent her brother a fond look. "Perhaps an orphanage and a hospital, supported by wealthy and powerful patrons. There's little help for those afflicted with... *challenges*."

Often no help at all. If they were lucky enough to be born into a family of means, they were shuttled off to the country, hidden away their entire lives.

She closed her eyes and rested her head in the corner of the chair. "Just imagine. A school for children like Chris and a hospital, too. Why, you could treat patients there." Slowly, her lashes fluttered open, and he could almost grasp her dream.

Watching the cavorting flames, he idly rubbed his thumb and forefinger together. "I ken several people willin' to support such a cause, includin' Yvette McTavish."

Sarah perked up. "Truly?"

He nodded and shifted his attention to her. "I forgot to tell ye. Yvette and Ewan should arrive in London within the week." He slapped his knees. "I say we propose such a venture to them."

THE NEXT AFTERNOON, just as Sarah finished sewing a button onto Gregor's greatcoat, the bell ringing below revealed clients had entered Stapleton Shipping and Supplies. As she had the past three days, she checked that the bolt securing the door was in place, and on silent feet, rushed to keep Chris quiet.

"*Shh.*" She shook her head, one finger to her lips as her heart beat a hard, staccato rhythm. "You cannot play with your toys right now, Chris."

"'Cause we're hiding from Satan and the bad men still?"

"That's right, darling." She squatted beside him.

A bewildered scowl pulled his mouth down. "Sister, why do they want to hurt us?"

"I don't know." She had an inkling why, however.

Gregor's voice echoed in the stairwell, his deep brogue, now quite familiar and always welcome. He knocked softly two times rapidly, followed by a single rap—the signal that all was well.

Giving her brother a reassuring smile, she patted her hair and ran her rough hands down the front of her gown. Until now—until Gregor—she hadn't cared all that much about her appearance. Her clothing and hairstyle had been practical, serviceable, and kept her gender hidden.

That was what had been important. Was what had kept them alive.

But now...

She couldn't lie to herself. She wanted to appear pretty, but without pins, she could do little with her hair but plait it. And while the gown she wore was a vast improvement over her shoddy boy's attire, it fell far short of attractive, and the fit was dismal at best.

Chris resumed playing with his toy soldiers, his tongue caught between his lower teeth as he hummed to himself. What would become of him if she couldn't retrieve the chest and her grandmother didn't come 'round?

Cat, regally perched nearby, observed Chris's every move. The furry imp reached his paw out and batted a soldier over. Then another. He looked at Chris, blinked his big green eyes, and knocked over a third soldier.

Chris burst out laughing, and a gratified smile swept Sarah's mouth upward. It had been so long since he'd been this happy.

The door swung open, and Gregor stepped through, a look on his face she'd come to recognize meant he had another surprise. He quite liked surprises.

Behind him, filed in three of the most elegant women Sarah had ever laid eyes upon.

"Blimey," Chris breathed, his jaw practically banging his chest.

Cat, on the other hand, appeared entirely unimpressed. After one bored, superior glance, he lifted a paw to his mouth —the same paw used to attack the soldiers—and begin grooming.

Chris's awed gaze flicked from lady to lady to lady then returned to Sarah. He stood and tried to smooth his thick, newly trimmed hair. "Coo, I ain't never seen the like afore, sister."

Trying not to wince at the slang he'd picked up while in London, Sarah corrected his grammar. "You haven't ever seen the like, Chris."

"That's what I just said. They're prettier than angels straight from heaven, aren't they?" As if he'd a notion of what angels looked like.

Gregor chuckled, and for some illogical reason, Sarah stifled the urge to tell him to hush. If she'd felt inferior a few moments ago, compared to these polished diamonds, she felt like a ragged beggarwoman now.

Not a hair out of place, their ensembles resembling

garments straight from an Ackermann fashion plate, they whisked into the room, their friendly smiles only partially putting Sarah at ease.

"Allow me to introduce ye," Gregor said, pride shining in his eyes the color of the sky before a storm.

Nine

Sarah permitted Gregor to draw her forward, kindness and understanding softening his face.

For the first time in her life, she wished the floor might swallow her up. Mustering every ounce of fortitude she possessed, she forced her mouth into a polite smile. It wasn't these lovely women's fault she lacked confidence or felt entirely out of her element. She mightn't be able to do a thing about her attire, but rag-mannered she'd not be.

In truth, she ought to be thanking them profusely for coming at all.

"Sarah, this is Her Grace, Alexandra, Duchess of Harcourt." Gregor motioned to an exotic black-haired beauty wearing a violet gown and spencer trimmed with ebony lace and velvet. "Adaira, Countess of Clarendon." He indicated the petite woman, resplendent in a pale blue traveling suit. "And, Isobel, Countess of Ramsbury."

The latter, attired in a soft plum and cream striped redingote, was possibly the most beautiful woman Sarah had ever seen. Even she couldn't help but stare.

Practically beaming, Gregor completed the introductions.

"Your Grace, my ladies, may I present Sarah Paine and her brother, Christopher?"

"Mums." Chris attempted a courtier's bow, earning him delighted cries and claps from the ladies.

Where had he learned to do that?

Ah, the other day when Gregor had bowed to her.

A credit to their kindness, none of the ladies mentioned his incorrect form of address. Likely Gregor had explained Chris's special needs as well as the complete lack of interaction the Paines had ever had with aristocrats.

"I am honored, Your Grace, your ladyships. I regret you've been discomposed on my behalf." Sarah curtsied, and as she rose in one lithe movement, couldn't prevent sending Gregor a triumphant smile.

Yes, she'd been practicing too.

He gave the subtlest wink of approval, and that lovely, addicting heat, like sweetened warm chocolate, spiraled outward from her middle.

The duchess made a shooing motion, her astute gaze inspecting Sarah from her braided hair to her scuffed shoes and saggy stockings, clearly visible beneath the too-short gown. "You must call me Alexa. Any friend of Gregor's is a friend of mine."

He had told them she was his friend?

Sarah wasn't confident that was a good thing, given the acute curiosity the ladies' genial smiles and friendly greetings couldn't entirely hide. Surely, they didn't think...?

Oh, God.

Did they believe she was a *special* friend to him?

One of a less than reputable nature?

No. No, she reassured herself. They wouldn't be here if they did. So how, precisely, had Gregor explained their relationship? She tossed him a considering look.

"Yes, please do call me, Addy," the Countess of Clarendon

insisted, scrunching her nose in a winsome fashion. "I'm seldom addressed as Adaira."

"Aye, 'tis true and generally only when she's been embroiled in mischief of some sort," Gregor said, grinning, his tone light and teasing like a beloved sibling. "For instance, abductin' a laird of the realm. A certain earl known for his rigid adherence to decorum."

"Never say you did?" Sarah reassessed the small woman. Wasn't she the one who raised prize horses too? She might well have to rethink everything she'd previously believed about nobility.

Addy's wink was nothing short of vixenish. "I did, but it was a colossal misunderstanding. And in the end, Clarendon fell madly in love with me." She rolled a dainty shoulder. "So, all's well that ends well."

Her sister, the Countess of Ramsbury, studied Sarah, her intelligent gaze contemplative. "Sarah, what Alexa says is true. Gregor's word is enough for us. You've no need to worry in that regard, and do call me Isobel."

Sarah didn't know what to say.

Ladies didn't go about giving permission for commoners to address them by their first names.

Mayhap she'd underestimated Gregor's position. Lord, had she insulted him by doing so? Her mind raced to recall any incident when she'd been less than respectful. *Dash it all.* Since the moment she plowed into his office, she'd treated him as her equal. He'd never indicated she should do otherwise.

The duchess glided forward and clasped Sarah's hand. "My dear, we are going to be the greatest of friends. I know it. Now, gather your things. We are going shopping."

The countesses bobbed their bonneted heads in agreement, eyes alight with excitement, and looking quite proud of themselves. Why, they were enjoying this intrigue.

Sarah sought Gregor's gaze. "Isn't that dangerous? For me to go out, I mean?"

The Countess of Clarendon—Addy—wandered to the window and peered at the dock below. "We alighted from a carriage out front, but we'll leave in one of the two waiting behind the building."

The duchess grinned, a twinkle in her eyes. "We need you suitably dressed for your first foray into society. I'm delighted to say, your grandmother has accepted an invitation to tea Monday next."

Sarah's heart stuttered. She believed she had until Christmas—almost three weeks—to prepare to meet her grandmother. But next Monday?

Ten short—*very short*—days?

Another unwelcome thought brought her up short. Just how much was this going to cost?

Too much.

She'd never been a gambler, and she wasn't certain spending money she couldn't spare on garments to impress Lady Rolandson was a wager she would win.

Adaira crossed to Chris. "I should very much like you to meet my children, Chris. My boys would be delighted for the company. You are of an age, I believe."

"May I, Sister?" Chris's countenance glowed from excitement. He'd never had a friend. Not even at Bellewood House.

Her gaze warm and welcoming, Adaira came to stand before Sarah. Several inches shorter, her height in no way diminished her presence.

"We've discussed it." Her vibrant eyes took in Gregor, Alexa, and Isobel. "If you're in agreement, Gregor will escort Chris to my house to play with my children while you, Alexa, and Isobel go shopping."

Chris would adore that.

"Afterward," Adaira said, "my husband and I would be honored if you and your brother would agree to stay with us until things are settled with Lady Rolandson. If it becomes a lengthy process, we'd be delighted to celebrate Christmas and Twelfth Night with you, too. My husband and I host an annual Yuletide Ball, and I vow, no one makes a better plum-pudding than Cook."

Mama had always made plum pudding on Stir-Up Sunday. She'd even gathered local greenery and made a sort of tropical kissing bough.

A tiny spark of discomfit gave Sarah pause. Or perchance, others taking control of her life was what disconcerted her most. She must entrust herself and her brother to women she'd just met on the advice of a man she scarcely knew any better. It wasn't easy to let go. To put her faith in strangers when she'd relied solely on herself for so long.

Isobel must've noticed her hesitation. "We only want to help, Sarah, and you needn't concern yourself with the cost. Consider the purchase our Christmastide gift to someone we would like to bless as we've been blessed."

Sarah swallowed against the tightness constricting her throat. Kindness such as this had been rare these past few years. Though it bordered on impudent, she must have an answer. "You don't know me; why would you extend such generosity?"

"Because Gregor asked us to." The Duchess of Harcourt lifted a hand toward the Scot solemnly observing the exchange. "And we have absolute trust in him and his judgment."

That said much about Gregor, that these women loved and respected him.

I could, too.

She firmly tamped down the unbidden thought. This may be the chance that she had prayed for. Mayhap her only chance. Neither pride nor fear would prevent her from accepting their benevolence.

Yes, she'd go to the fittings. She'd allow the ladies to purchase her clothing, and pray that her grandmother would reimburse their expenses. If the Dowager Viscountess Rolandson still refused to acknowledge her grandchildren—

Well, Sarah wouldn't deny Chris one last, wonderful Yuletide.

Beyond that, she couldn't contemplate. The near future gleamed brightly, and what lay beyond that glow, she'd fret about when she must.

She stepped nearer to Adaira, and after a swift glance toward Chris, assuring he'd returned to his toys and wouldn't hear her, lowered her voice. "No doubt you've noticed Chris has some challenges. Are you certain you're comfortable taking him?"

Such an incredulous expression swept the countess's face that Sarah was at once ashamed.

"I understand and admire your concern for your brother, Sarah. That makes you a caring sister. But I promise you Chris will be treated with the utmost respect and gentleness. Gregor mentioned Chris's love of horses, too. I have the gentlest pony that my sons ride. With your permission, I'd like to teach Chris to ride, as well."

Chris might never be adept at the sport, but at least he'd be allowed to try. He wasn't supposed to be able to walk either, but his tenacity proved the doctor wrong. Given the opportunity, who knew what he could do?

Once again, Sarah must rely on her woman's instinct, and though she admitted to being anxious, no alarm tunneled through her veins. Her nape hair didn't stand on end, nor did her stomach wobble in fear. Giving a slight nod, she acquiesced. "Very well. Thank you, and Chris would love to learn to ride."

Relief softened the corners of Gregor's eyes. Had he really thought she'd put up a fuss? Something like sorrow also deepened his eyes to slate blue. Was he saddened as much as she to part?

She'd miss him. Much more than she ought to after a mere three-day acquaintance. But Mama swore she'd known she'd loved Papa after their third meeting.

Love?

Was it possible to fall in love so quickly? Affection and interest—those were feasible. Even physical desire. But love?

No.

What about Mama and Papa?

They'd been devoted to each other, and if Mama ever regretted leaving her privileged lifestyle for that of the ship captain's wife, she never breathed a hint. It mattered not whether her parents had been in love. Sarah didn't have time for such distractions. Everything she did was to ensure Chris's future.

In short order, her few possessions, along with Chris and his toys, had been bundled into one of the waiting coaches accompanied by the lovely Countess of Clarendon.

Sarah couldn't contain her surprise at how readily her brother had accepted Adaira's hand, and after a fond kiss on his forehead had been led from Gregor's apartment.

"I'll ride with the lad to Clarendons', just in case he needs a familiar face." Gregor draped a cloak around Sarah's shoulders. Likely another castoff from the charity bin. He handed her a plain straw poke bonnet.

"We'll wait for you in the carriage, Sarah." Alexa exchanged a telling look with Isobel.

Had they detected the undercurrent of attraction between her and Gregor?

Of course, it was only natural that she felt gratitude toward him, and perhaps it had become infatuation, as well.

She'd been most careful to hide her interest, and she believed she'd done a satisfactory job.

Now wasn't the time for flirtations or romantic entanglements.

Would there ever be a time?

She'd faced that disconcerting truth some time ago. It would take an extraordinary man to win her heart. Because he must accept that Chris would always be a part of their lives. Few men—none that she knew aside from Papa—would willingly take on such a burden.

Except for Gregor jesting about accepting a kiss in repayment, he'd been the perfect gentleman. She'd been the one who agreed to the terms and could not fault him in that regard.

"Thank you, Gregor. For everything."

He rested a hand on her shoulder, giving it a gentle squeeze. His voice slightly husky, and his brogue a trace thicker, he said, "It's been my pleasure, lass."

More emotional about their inevitable separation than she would've anticipated, Sarah struggled against tears. Eyes lowered, she managed a short nod.

"Nae tears, *jo*."

No tears, she silently chastised herself.

He lifted her chin and swept a thumb across her damp cheek. "I promise ye, I'm no' desertin' ye. I vowed to see ye safely settled, and I am goin' to keep my oath." He flashed his charming grin. "Besides, Adaira invited me to dinner tonight."

Sarah smiled wide, uncaring he might guess why. "You've already done so much for us. I truly don't expect any more—"

"The truth is, I've enjoyed yer company, and I'll miss ye. Promise ye'll let me take ye on an outin' to Hyde Park tomorrow."

"All right." How could she say no?

He raised her hand, pressing a kiss to her knuckles, and a

jolt of sensation streaked to her elbow then skittered up her shoulder.

This was a man she could care for. A man she'd risk much for. But there was Chris to consider.

Gregor pivoted her toward the door. "Now go, before they parade back up here to see what the delay is."

"I owe ye a kiss." On impulse, she stood on her toes, laid a palm against the broad plane of his chest, and touched her lips to his.

At first, he remained rigid and unmoving. Then with a groan deep in his chest, he urged her close and kissed her like a man long-starved. Breathing heavily, he angled away and growled, "Go. Now. Before I canna let ye."

With a last glance over her shoulder and a small wave, she turned her back, feeling almost as desolate as she had when fleeing Jamaica. Fighting tears and struggling to compose herself, she slipped into the coach.

The duchess patted the seat beside her. "Sit here, my dear."

Sarah sank onto the plush bird's egg-blue seat, and Alexa wrapped her kid gloved fingers 'round Sarah's.

Isobel fished a delicate lace handkerchief from her reticule and passed the square across the carriage. She met Alexa's eyes as she settled into the squabs and put a finger to her chin. "I don't believe I've ever seen Gregor so entranced."

Sarah raised a startled glance. "I beg your pardon?"

"Leave it to us." Alexa patted her hand. "We'll have him coming 'round in no time."

TEN

Three days later, Gregor handed his hat to Ramsbury's majordomo.

Today, he'd been invited to a proper English tea. Hadn't he become the simpering fop? He brushed a cat hair off his buff coat. He reserved it, and the cherry and shimmering gold waistcoat he wore, for special occasions. What could be more special than seeing Sarah Paine again?

The three days since they'd parted felt like three interminable months. He'd thought of her continuously, had written to her daily, and his apartment was unbearably quiet and lonely now.

Cat even wandered around meowing plaintively.

The much-anticipated outing with her to Hyde Park had not manifested. After dinner at the Clarendon's, he'd returned home to find his living quarters ransacked. It hadn't taken a good deal of thought to figure out who was behind the break-in.

Yesterday, he'd interrogated Mrs. Smith, and the housekeeper tearfully confessed she'd seen a toy soldier beneath the couch when she last cleaned Gregor's quarters. A little more probing, and she admitted to accepting a few coins for sharing that tidbit with a scruffy, bearded man.

Yeates.

Mrs. Smith didn't think sharing that morsel would hurt anything, for she'd seen no other evidence of anything out of the ordinary. Her unfortunate choice had earned her a dismissal, but Gregor had conceded to provide her with a reference and a purse to hold her over until she found another position.

A locksmith had been retained, and not only did Stapleton Shipping and Supplies now have new locks throughout, he'd hired two former soldiers to patrol the perimeter.

Thank God, Sarah and Chris had already left. He shuddered to think what would've happened had they been discovered.

Voices and laughter filtered from the drawing room. Having been here a few times before, he motioned for the butler to answer the new knock sounding at the door.

"I ken the way."

"Excellent, sir."

Gregor lingered in the drawing room entrance, taking a few moments to savor his friends, family, and, most of all, Sarah enjoying themselves. Previous visits had taught him that this room, as well as the rest of the house, would be decked out in holiday gaiety come Christmas Eve. Likely a few days beforehand since Isobel adored the holiday.

Wearing a lavender gown, a delicate lace fichu tucked into the bodice—unfortunately hiding the creamy bounty within —and amethyst and pearl earrings dangling from her dainty earlobes, Sarah looked every bit the lady of refinement. Her hair twisted into an intricate knot, she held a yellow chintz-patterned teacup as she smiled and made polite conversation.

A queer sensation kicked behind his ribs. *Gude,* he'd missed her. Missed her laugh and ready smile. Missed the gentle interaction with her brother. Missed her keen intellect, droll retorts, and the way her eyes rounded in wonder. He even missed the way her nose crinkled when he said something in Scots or Gaelic that she didn't understand but was too polite to say so.

How had she and Chris wiggled their ways into his heart so quickly?

Ewan vowed he loved Yvette the minute he danced with her, but it had been two years before they met again.

Isobel spied him and glided to the door. She looped her hand through the crook of his elbow and drew him forward. "I had begun to think you weren't coming, and that I'd misread your fascination with our dear Sarah."

Just what did she mean by that? He gave her a shrewd assessment, but she'd already turned away, leading him straight to Sarah.

Had he been that bloody obvious? Pointing his gaze ceilingward, he stifled unfamiliar chagrin. By God, he hadn't moped about like a moon-eyed milksop. He'd not even hinted his interest, so how did Isobel and the others know?

Women seemed to have an extra sense about these matters.

He knew the instant Sarah realized he stood beside her, though she hadn't glanced in his direction.

The faintest flush pinkened her cheeks, and she carefully set her teacup upon the table, before turning a radiant smile upon him. "Hello, Mr. McTavish."

How odd to have her address him so formally, but she'd not want to give rise to tattle. "Always a pleasure, Miss Paine." He inclined his head.

Lord and Lady Warrick entered the drawing room, and Isobel floated away to greet them.

Gregor eyed the dainty chair, the only remaining vacant seat near Sarah. He could either perch like an oversized bird upon its edge or remain standing. For he hadn't a doubt that if he applied his full weight to the flimsy thing, the legs would give way, and he'd land on his arse.

Isobel clapped her hands, and her husband, Yancy, Earl of Ramsbury, joined her, and with a doting smile, she placed a hand on his forearm. "I have something special to show you." She gave the callers a mysterious smile. "Please follow me."

A swift perusal of the guests had Gregor's mouth twitching at the corners. Everyone, yes, every last one, was married except for him and Sarah.

So, the grand ladies—*and their husbands?*—played match-makers, did they? Not subtly either, by God. He ought to have considered that he'd set himself up for their interference when he asked them to help a young woman of his acquaintance. Interestingly though, he didn't mind.

Nae, he didn't mind at all.

Adaira caught his eye and whispered something in Clarendon's ear. The earl gave Gregor an apologetic shrug before guiding his wife from the room. Aye, the chaps were involved, too. Likely inveigled into assisting their meddling wives.

On cue, the other couples filed from the room, leaving Gregor and Sarah to come last.

He mightn't have objections, but their disregard for her feelings rankled a jot. What if she noticed their ploy? Would she be offended? Humiliated? He offered Sarah his elbow, and she placed her gloved hand upon it.

"I received your note about the break-in, Gregor. I hope you were able to restore everything to order."

He couldn't prevent the satisfied curving of his mouth that she deemed to use his given name when others were out of earshot. Her perfume, mild, floral, a hint spicy with a touch of citrus, wafted upward. Had she borrowed the scent, or had his cousins purchased it for her?

"Aye, and I've added extra security, as well," he said.

Another waft of fragrance floated past. He almost bent to smell her shiny hair. Had she used scented soap to wash it? He reluctantly towed his errant thoughts back to the matter at hand.

"No doubt a good idea," she murmured a bit distractedly.

"Sarah, I believe Santano's thugs are still watchin' the offices, and I'd like to set a trap for them with yer permission, lass." He slowed their progress.

"A trap?" She cut a swift glance at those entering the conservatory.

Was she worried about the propriety of being alone with him? Now? When they'd spent days together? Well, Chris had always been there, but still…

"Aye." No help for it. He must speak with her privately, and this was likely his only opportunity. He drew her to a halt. "I hope to apprehend the scoundrel before he sails. Several of the gentlemen in attendance here today are meetin' me at White's this afternoon to discuss the plan. But I wanted ye to be aware first. Do ye have any idea why he pursues ye, *jo*?"

Her tongue darted out to wet her lower lip, and she tucked her chin, causing her earrings to sway.

As he'd suspected, she'd been keeping something from him.

"I do. I possess a key my mother gave me. I believe it belongs to a chest hidden at Bellewood." She cut him a swift, almost guilty glance before continuing. "That is—was—our home in Jamaica. I don't know what the chest contains, but my father showed it to me once and told me it was to ensure Chris's future. I can only presume the contents are of some value. I also don't know if Santano assumes I have the chest here and believes I've hidden it somewhere. I don't think he's found it yet because he wouldn't continue to plague me otherwise."

"He must know what it contains then, and I'd wager the

contents are precious." Gregor placed his hand over hers and gently squeezed her fingers. "What if we were to use another chest as bait?"

He squinted in concentration. Greedy sods like Santano lusted after wealth. Setting a snare for him and his henchmen shouldn't be all that difficult.

"Do you really think it would work?" Such hope lit Sarah's face, he longed to wrap her in his arms, pull her close, and assure her it would

He didn't dare, standing in the corridor, more was the pity.

Someday though...

"I do. Is that why he killed yer parents?"

Pain tightened her features, and the long, graceful column of her throat worked. "He killed my father for control of the *Mary Elizabeth*. I believe he may have killed my mother trying to find the chest, though I don't know that for certain."

"Sarah?" Placing his hands on her upper arms, Gregor turned her to face him. "Are you saying your mother might be alive?"

"Oh, Gregor." Her eyes glistened, her pain tearing at his heart. "I want it to be so with all my heart. But there hasn't been a word in three years. I keep hoping she's written my grandmother or could somehow make her way to England. But Mama was sickly when she forced Chris and me to leave her behind. If it hadn't been for Chris, I would've refused to go."

And she'd probably be dead now.

Gregor gathered her into his embrace and kissed the top of her head. Devil take what anybody had to say. Not knowing whether her mother lived or not must eat away like a serrated, rusting blade every day.

"Lass, I ken ships that sail to the Caribbean—specifically Jamaica. I can have inquiries made so that ye'll know once and for all about yer mother." He dared press his mouth to her silky, fragrant hair again. "It might bring ye peace."

She deserved peace. Deserved to have someone take care of her for a change.

Eyes closed, her breathing ragged, and head bowed, she struggled for control. At last, she whispered, "I want to know. I cannot ever find peace until I do."

"I'll see to it at once then."

Weighty silence filled the passageway.

Memories likely flooded Sarah's thoughts while Gregor calculated his next step. Clarendon, Warrick, and Ewan had worked as spies for the Home Office. He didn't doubt they'd have a shrewd idea or two that could help lead to Santano's capture and imprisonment.

A thought struck, and he asked, "Can ye prove yer father's ownership of the *Mary Elizabeth*?"

"Yes. I have the documentation. Mama thought to send it with me and the deed to Bellewood, too. But I expect Santano possessed forged documents claiming the ship is his."

Not hard to disprove with the right influence and resources, both of which Gregor had access to.

She'd been incredibly brave, very much like the women he'd introduced her to the other day. Someday, she'd have to hear their stories. He'd be bound, she would never believe the Duchess of Harcourt had once been a Highland gypsy. Or that Alexa had helped Isobel escape the band of rogue Highlanders who abducted her.

Aye, introducin' her to these braw, bonnie women is wise.

"While we have a moment alone, I wanted to invite ye to the theater tomorrow night." Gregor had no idea what the performance was, but every one of the lords now chatting in the conservatory had private boxes. For the second time in less than a week, he meant to take advantage of those connections. "And also if ye're agreeable, the Christmas Pantomime on

Drury Lane on Boxin' Day, as well as Astley's Christmas Spectacular. Chris is welcome, too, of course."

"I've never been to any of them. They sound wonderful." She'd regained her composure, and a half-smile curved her mouth. "I'm not sure Chris would appreciate the theater, but he so adores horses. I'm certain he'd enjoy Astley's."

Yancy poked his head around the door, cocking a reproving eyebrow at Gregor. "Are you coming? Isobel has a special surprise, just for Miss Paine."

"Aye." He took Sarah's elbow. Still far too thin. "Come along, *jo*."

"*Jo*? What does that mean?" Her bright eyes brimming with curiosity, she searched his face.

"Sweetheart or darlin'."

"Oh." Instead of blushing or dropping her gaze in a maidenly fashion, she grinned, joy blossoming across her face.

Gregor couldn't suppress a slightly smug smile.

Upon entering the lush plant and flower-filled room, she released a delighted cry. Several parakeets flitted about, but it was the elaborate cage containing two green parrots that had her flying across the tiled floor.

"Oh, stars. They are yellow-billed parrots. Just like those in Jamaica."

"They are," Isobel agreed. "I acquired them a month ago from a traveling showman. They weren't being cared for well. When Gregor mentioned you'd had a pet one in Jamaica, I knew I had to introduce you before moving them to our country aviary."

"I confess, they make me homesick." Sarah gripped the cage, resting her forehead on the wires, a hint of sorrow shadowing her features.

Isobel pressed Sarah's hand. "You are welcome to visit them anytime while they are still here, and once we've moved them to the aviary, as well."

"Isobel studies all manner of species of birds and other things." Gregor caught Ramsbury's attention. "Might I make use of yer theater box tomorrow? Miss Paine has agreed to attend with me."

More hearty approval followed his announcement. Because they were excited about the performance or that he'd asked Sarah to accompany him? The latter to be sure, for he'd not mentioned which theater. The performance might've been the rotund Prince Regent dancing naked atop a pink elephant, and they'd have agreed if only to see the courtship's progression.

As Gregor had anticipated, all present invited themselves along.

Rather than look overwhelmed, Sarah seemed pleased.

He was too, but not only because her happiness brought him joy.

Shortly, he'd put the plan in place he'd spent days contriving. With Sarah's key and a fake chest as bait, Santano would soon be in the authorities' hands.

Eleven

Sitting in the Ramsburys' private box in the opulent Theatre Royal Drury Lane, Sarah scarcely knew what the current entertainment on stage was about. After the first performance—a rather depressing tragedy—the audience was now treated to a pantomime.

She didn't dare say so, but she found his antics more silly than humorous.

From the boisterous chortles and feminine titters, she might be alone in her observation, though from the sideways peeks she'd sent Gregor, he appeared more appalled than anything else.

A comedy now had the glittering crowd hooting and hollering. Those who weren't spying on others with their opera glasses, that was. However, as he had all evening, the riveting man at her side commandeered her attention.

She glanced down, smoothing her hand over the beautiful satin. As the garments commissioned for her wouldn't be ready for at least another week, she wore a gown borrowed from the Duchess of Harcourt. Sarah had never felt more regale Or more unequivocally out of place—as if she play-acted and pretended to be someone, something, she wasn't.

Every aspect of this seemed wrong on some level.

Why couldn't she just be Sarah, daughter of Captain and Mrs. Aaron Paine from Jamaica? Wasn't that good enough?

No. Not if she was to get into her grandmother's good graces. At this point, she wasn't even sure that was what she wanted anymore.

Gregor was her steadying rudder through it all, and her heart ached to think that soon they may go their separate ways. Scarcely over a week ago, panic had propelled her into his office. Now her circumstances were vastly improved, but every bit of the change was due, at least in part, to him.

His thoughtfulness. His connections. His perseverance. His goodness.

Seated on the far end of the box, every now and again, he ran his finger over the back of her hand resting in her lap. Brazen, considering the candles remained lit in their box. Only a few private boxes had extinguished their tapers.

Surely, everyone sitting nearby heard her heart knocking against her breastbone.

This gruff—much too attractive for her own good—Highlander was well on his way to capturing her heart.

Nonetheless, as long as Santano searched for her and Chris, she could never relax, never let down her guard. She couldn't be confident of their safety, even with a warrior like Gregor and his influential friends vowing their protection. They couldn't know Santano was pure evil, and he seemed to have spies everywhere.

This evening as she descended from the coach, she'd caught sight of a vaguely familiar, shadowy figure lurking across the street from the theater. She couldn't be sure, of course. Not with poor lighting and her hurried glimpse. But something about his bearing caused her nape hairs to rise, and her instinct screamed danger.

Perhaps she was paranoid, but only a fool failed to be cautious and dismissed something like that as chance. On the way home, she'd discuss her concerns with Gregor. For now, she'd enjoy his company and the rather awful performance upon the stage.

She squinted, leaning forward a couple of inches. Was that a man dressed as a buxom woman?

Gregor bent near, touching her hand again and whispering in her ear. "Enjoyin' yerself, lass?"

How could something as innocent as touching hands heighten her awareness of him? "Yes. Very much." Not because of the actors on the stage, however. No, another captured her interest. Feeling incredibly daring, she laid her other hand atop his and squeezed his fingers.

He boldly returned the caress.

Someone behind them cleared her throat, and she withdrew her hand. Either they'd been caught in their indiscretion, or fate had intervened and brought her to her senses.

Encouraging him was unwise, as was indulging her growing infatuation. In a matter of days, she'd meet her grandmother at the duchess's tea, and Sarah would know one way or the other whether she and Chris would remain in London or move elsewhere.

She'd already conceived new identities for her brother and her, should the need arise, and she wouldn't hesitate to flee once again. Even if that meant not telling these kindhearted people where she was going. Much depended upon the success of the scheme Gregor and his friends had concocted to entrap Santano.

An hour later, as they left the theater, the men sheltered the women from the curious onlookers and an occasional drunken reveler. His features stern and posture tense, Gregor guided her to the waiting carriages. "Look lively, lads. I've an uneasy feelin'."

So did she.

Even as the words left his mouth, Santano's three thugs rushed from the crowd directly toward her. Gregor neatly stepped in front of her, dispatching Yeates with a mighty blow to his jaw.

He dropped to the pavement like a soiled handkerchief.

Lords Clarendon and Ramsbury wrestled the smaller ruffian to the ground, but the third escaped.

Her heart pounding her throat, Sarah stared into Santano's hireling's hate-filled face, as he thrashed in the lordships' arms.

"Santano knows where you're stayin', bitch. Best be sayin' your prayers—"

Another well-placed punch from Gregor rendered him unconscious, as well.

Sarah clutched Gregor's arm. "Chris!"

"Ramsbury, will ye see these bloody rotters are arrested?" Gregor asked as he handed her into the carriage.

"With immense pleasure." Ramsbury signaled his driver. The strapping fellow and Harcourt's drivers were binding the attackers' wrists and ankles as Sarah's conveyance pulled away from the throng.

Less than thirty minutes later, after a harrowing ride, her nerves tattered raw from worry, she closed Chris's bedchamber door. The servants assured her and Lord and Lady Clarendon that nothing out of the ordinary had transpired in their absence.

Allowing Gregor to lead her downstairs, Sarah pulled her shawl tighter about her shoulders. "Do you think Santano really knows we are here?"

Gregor drew her to halt, turning her so that she faced him. "It's no' only possible, we want him to ken. As an extra precaution, I'll be stayin' here 'til the scunner's caught." His mouth quirked in that roguish manner she'd come to know. "Just think, *jo,* I can give ye more dancin' lessons."

Excitement and alarm swept her, not only that he would stay here, but that he'd tried sweeping her worry aside and changing the subject. She crossed her arms. "I presume you're going to explain those statements to me?"

"Dinna get yer feathers ruffled, lass. I'm no' keepin' secrets from ye." He kissed her forehead, right there for all to see, as if he were staking a claim on her. For a blissful instant, she forgot her fear.

Only an instant though before reality crashed upon her senses. "Good try, Highlander." She poked his chest. "I'll have the truth of it, and don't spare my sensibilities. In case you haven't noticed, I'm not a delicate flower or a swooning sort of female."

"Aye." He gave her a scorching glance that sent a frisson along her spine. "I noticed that about ye, and a lot more too." He made slow work of raking his gaze over her from head to toe and back again.

"Gregor McTavish!" She didn't sound half so outraged as flattered at his seductive smile and the rakish glint hooding his turbulent gaze.

"Och, dinna fash yerself." He tapped her nose. "Today, word was deliberately spread around the places Santano, and his sailors frequent that soon after my apartment was searched, a chest was delivered to Stapleton Shippin' and Supplies. If all goes as planned, Santano will attempt to steal it. Given I've added new security measures, I'm positive he'll take the bait. Once inside the warehouse, he'll find much more than a chest awaits him."

His low, slightly wicked chuckle sent shivers scuttling along her shoulders. Gregor McTavish wasn't a man to underestimate.

A FEW DAYS LATER, Sarah inhaled a steadying breath and swallowed her nerves as she and Gregor entered the Harcourts' grand house. After passing the butler her new navy-blue silk bonnet and velvet-lined pelisse, she commanded her frolicking pulse to calm. As it was wont to do, the unruly thing completely ignored her dictate.

She must do this.

With Gregor by her side, she could.

"Has Lady Rolandson arrived yet, Tibbs?" Sarah couldn't wait an instant longer to ask the question burning the tip of her tongue.

"Yes, Miss Paine." The butler accepted Gregor's cane and hat, as well.

She would've preferred to meet her grandmother for the first time in a private setting, but her ladyship's refusal to so much as speak to her had brought this public confrontation upon herself.

It had actually been quite brilliant of Alexa, truth to tell.

Gripping Gregor's arm as if it were a lifeline, Sarah allowed him to guide her down the passageway. Catching sight of them as they passed an ornate gilded mirror, a tiny smile bent her mouth. If she didn't know better, she'd suspect he'd picked his blue tartan waistcoat because it matched her midnight blue gown.

Both tall and blond, they did, indeed, make a most attractive couple. Their children would be blond too, no doubt. Would their offspring have his blue-gray eyes or her hazel ones?

If only it might be so.

Those ruminations would have to wait. Her future was but a few feet away, and she intended to face it head-on. She squared her shoulders, stiffened her spine, and elevated her chin.

Mustering her composure, and ordering whatever the rambunctious creatures frolicking in her middle were to settle down, Sarah permitted Gregor to lead her into the drawing room.

"Smile, lass." He squeezed her arm. "Ye look like ye're goin' to a funeral. What's the worst that can happen?"

She was, in essence, facing a sort of death. For today she'd either forge a new future or slam the door on her past forever. As for the worst that could happen? Well, she wasn't sure where Gregor fit in either of those scenarios, and she very much wanted him to. Very much, indeed.

He winked in that confident manner that never failed to charm a smile from her. "Ye and Chris can always come to Scotland with me."

Eyes narrowed the merest bit, she took his measure. Did he jest, or was he sincere? Then her mind stumbled upon the truth, and dismay bludgeoned her. "You're returning to Scotland?"

"Aye," he agreed, his voice somewhat gravelly.

Dismay throttled up her throat. She'd become accustomed to his company. His dear face and roguish humor. And he was leaving.

"When?"

It wasn't any of her business. She'd hoped to see him after —that was *if*—things went well with her grandmother. Sarah lied to herself. She had counted on his being there, no matter the outcome. To think he wouldn't nearly undid her.

He rolled a shoulder nonchalantly. "It depends."

On what? She wanted to scream.

He canted his head in response to a handsome dark-haired man's greeting. "Yvette and Ewan are here, Sarah." He seemed inordinately pleased by that. "I'll introduce ye later."

With a small start, she realized who the man and the stunning blonde at his side were. Rumor had it, Yvette McTavish was the wealthiest woman in the whole of Britain. Sarah swept her gaze over the assembled guests, glittering in their high-fashion finery. Her grandmother was in this room somewhere.

She would have to wait to find out when Gregor intended to leave for Scotland. The moment she'd anticipated and dreaded was upon her. "I hope this isn't a colossal mistake," she whispered.

At once, Alexa glided to their sides.

Speaking quietly, she murmured, "Sarah, your grandmother is sitting by the window. I don't believe she saw you arrive, but I do have salts available in case she swoons." Her eyes crinkled in amusement. "She's known to do that regularly."

Just perfect. Temperamental, mean-spirited, sharp-tongued, unforgiving, and given to the vapors. Had the dowager any redeeming qualities?

Digging her fingers into Gregor's forearm, Sarah marshaled every ounce of poise she possessed as the duchess wended her way across the drawing room, smiling and nodding to guests as she swept past.

Elegant, her mien superior and self-important, Lady Rolandson, attired in black from her lace cap to her gloves, was engaged in conversation with another distinguished grand dame near her age, also swathed in black from her sophisticated turban to her beaded, slippered toes.

Upon their approach, Lady Rolandson gave a disinterested upward sweep of her sparse lashes. Eyes widening, she froze, going perfectly still. The color draining from her face, she clutched at her throat as if choking. "Mary?"

Sarah shook her head, sinking onto the empty chair and offering a tremulous upward turn of her mouth. "No, I'm her daughter, Sarah Paine."

Almost at once, a plumpish prune-faced woman, perhaps in her fifth decade, rushed to her ladyship's side. Placing a hand on her shoulder, she patted gently, while glaring daggers at Sarah. "Calm yourself, Your Ladyship. Take deep breaths." All solicitous concern, she hovered above Grandmother. Rummaging in the reticule at her wrist, she asked, "Do you require your salts? 'Tis obvious *this person* has given you a most terrible upset."

Lady Rolandson speared the woman a sour look and shrugged the hand off her shoulder. "Stop coddling me, Bernice! You're my companion, not my nursemaid. I'll thank you to remember your place."

There was the temperamental harridan Sarah had been warned about.

Bernice's mouth cinched impossibly tighter as if she'd sucked a most unripe lemon. Something akin to fury tightened her plain features, and Sarah realized with an uncomfortable start, the companion's wrath was directed squarely at her. "But your heart, Your Ladyship," Bernice argued stiffly.

"Is now and has always been perfectly fine, *Miss Wattle*." After another scathing glance, Sarah's grandmother struggled to her feet, extending quaking hands. Eyes suspiciously moist, she offered a trembling smile. "My dear, why didn't you inform me you were in London? I'm beyond overcome, but so very delighted. I didn't even know of your existence."

Sarah stiffened, casting Gregor a flabbergasted look. It took all of her self-control not to condemn her grandmother for a liar right then and there. Was it possible he'd been right? That somehow, incredible as it seemed, her grandmother hadn't known about Sarah's many attempts to contact her?

With the slightest flexing of his eyes, he indicated she should go on.

Grandmother drew in a shaky breath, her focus sinking to

the floor. In a small, weak voice, she said, "These many years, I never heard from your mother. I'd given up hope."

"I beg your pardon?" Outrage at the blatant tarradiddle sluiced Sarah from her head to her toes curled tight in her slippers.

Gregor's heavy, soothing hand on her shoulder calmed her a mite.

"Not a word." Grandmother shook her head. "I'd hoped and prayed, as did Rolandson, that she'd contact us. For nearly ten years, I checked the post every day. I gave up after that, you see. It was just too painful..." Her eyes grew misty, and her chin quivered. A heartbroken, fragile old woman had replaced the formidable dowager of a few moments ago. She dabbed an eye with her knuckle. "I finally realized Mary would never be able to forgive me."

Miss Wattle made a *tutting* sound, her tone and gaze condemning. "I must say, you've some nerve, Miss Paine, showing up unannounced and distressing her ladyship in this matter. In public, too. For shame."

Who was this woman that she presumed order her and Grandmother about? Sarah bit the inside of her cheek from telling Miss Bernice Wattle precisely what she could do with her bloody disapproval. The suggestion might have something to do with a small body cavity.

"Might I advise you adjourn to a more private setting, my lady?" Alexa said as she cut Adaira a telling look.

The countess approached, concern pinching the corners of her eyes the merest bit.

Glancing around, Sarah encountered the curious glances of several other guests. Likely this gossip fodder would be whispered in drawing rooms and assemblies across London by day's end. It wasn't every day during a *le beau monde* tea that a peeress discovered the offspring she'd disowned decades before had a child.

Sarah's lips twitched. Grandmother might be allowed a fainting episode after all.

"Yes, yes, that would be wise, Your Grace. I should prefer to converse with my granddaughter alone." Lady Rolandson reached for Sarah's hand, and she reluctantly allowed the old woman to clasp it in her frail grasp.

Something was off here. Her grandmother didn't appear to be pretending her shock, so why would she claim that Mama had never written? Sarah possessed the returned letters.

"Yes, I too think it's wise to have this discussion in private and determine if this... *person* is who she claims she is. She might be impersonating your granddaughter in an attempt to swindle you." Accusation ringing in her words, Miss Wattle made to accompany them.

Balling a fist against the urge to slap the condescending smirk off Miss Wattle's chuffy face, Sarah forced herself to count to ten.

Gregor's hand lit upon her shoulder for a brief instant, once again calming her.

He *knew*. Knew how hard put Sarah was to bridle her tongue.

"Have you eyes in your empty head, Bernice?" Lady Rolandson swept a hand up and down Sarah. "She's the very image of her mother at that age, you twaddle-brain. You view Mary's portrait in the drawing room daily. Don't pretend you do not notice the resemblance," her ladyship snapped while leveling Miss Wattle a peevish glare.

"I believe grandmother and granddaughter should be permitted this reunion in private, Miss Wattle." Alexa's demeanor clearly expressed that nothing else was acceptable.

"But... I don't...What if...?" Miss Wattle stuttered.

"There's no need for you to join us," Grandmother said with a dismissive wave of her hand. "I expect our discussion to become quite emotional."

"I'm not sure you should be alone with *this person*, your ladyship. After all, we know absolutely nothing about her." Miss Wattle could be given credit for her tenacity, if not her ragged manners.

"Come, Miss Wattle." Adaira looped the vexed companion's arm through hers. "Have you met my brother, Lord Sethwick, and his lady?" Her side-eyed glance and slightly quirked mouth indicated she knew full well what Miss Wattle was about, and she wasn't having any of it.

"You won't leave, will you?" Sarah touched Gregor's arm.

"Nae. I'll be right here, waitin' for ye, *jo*." He crossed his arm over his chest. A gallant knight vowing his allegiance. "I swear."

TWELVE

Silently, Sarah and her grandmother followed Alexa down the corridor and into a charming sitting room decorated in shades of pale blue and peach.

"Shall I request tea for you?" Alexa asked.

Meeting her grandmother's hazel eyes, so very much like her own, Sarah shook her head "I don't care for any, but perhaps her ladyship would—"

"No, thank you, Your Grace." Still appearing somewhat stunned, Grandmother patted Sarah's hand and gave a weak smile.

"I'll leave you then." With a sympathetic meshing of her lips, Alexa swept from the room.

For a long, awkward moment, her head cocked in an almost robin-like fashion, Sarah's grandmother stared. "I cannot believe it. I simply cannot believe it. Oh, if Rolandson had only lived to see this day. He would've been so pleased. The resemblance to your mother is uncanny, my dear."

"Papa always said so, as well," Sarah admitted, feeling the familiar twist of her heart mentioning her beloved father brought.

Grandmother dashed a tear away from the corner of her eye, and a rather fragile smile replaced her drooping mouth. "I have a granddaughter."

"And grandson, too, my lady. His name is Christopher, he prefers Chris, and he's twelve years old." No need to tell her about Chris's difficulties just yet. She'd learn about them soon enough.

"Oh, my! A grandson." She clapped her hands once. "None of that *my lady* balderdash, either. I insist you call me Grandmama."

And, of course, no one told Lady Rolandson no.

Grandmama sank into a nearby chair, shaking her head back and forth, causing the jet earrings in her ears to sway with the motion. A few silvery curls peeked from beneath her crocheted cap. Had she been as blonde as Mama and her? Shoulders hunched, she put her hands to her face. "How I wish I could take back the harsh things I said to your mother," she sobbed. "My pride...My foolish, foolish pride and arrogance drove my darling daughter from me. I caused her to hate me." Her voice, sounding like ancient parchment, cracked. "She never once tried to contact me in all these years."

Unable to resist comforting the weeping woman, Sarah sank to her knees. This wasn't the callous harridan she'd believed her grandmother was.

Another great sob shook her frail shoulders.

"Mama *did* write to you. Many times. I have some of the unopened letters." She covered her grandmother's shaking shoulder. "Three years ago, Chris and I came to your house. We were turned away at the door. I wrote to you recently, just over a week ago, and that messenger was also turned away."

Grandmother collapsed back into the chair, her expression aghast, one hand clutching at her throat. "No. No. That's not possible." She shook her head so frantically, her cap slipped to one side. "No one told me," she gasped, her gaze bouncing around the room like marbles in a shaken cup.

Did she think Sarah lied?

"I swear, it's true. Gregor McTavish delivered the letter himself. We presumed you wanted nothing to do with us."

After a bit of fumbling, her grandmother pulled a delicate handkerchief from her bodice. She dried her face and blew her nose. At last, she managed, "I believe you, my dear. I do."

Remarkably pleased her grandmother should do so, Sarah's eyes misted.

An instant later, severe lines hardened Grandmother's lightly wrinkled face, giving Sarah a glimpse of the harsh woman she was reputed to be. Jerking upright, she slammed both palms onto the chair's arms. Forged steel replaced her earlier fragility. "That devious, conniving wench."

Sarah inched backward a jot, uncertain whether to admire or fear her grandmother. Lady Rolandson wasn't someone to cross. That much remained consistent with what she had heard about her grandmother.

Shrewdness narrowed the elderly woman's eyes. "Since Rolandson died and his nephew inherited the viscountcy, Bernice has hinted—quite regularly I might add—that I ought to leave her a generous settlement. You see, until you surprised me today, it was thought that I had no heirs to leave my personal wealth and holdings to. I simply refuse to let the Crown seize my monies, so unbeknownst to her, I bequeathed all but a stipend for her and the other servants to charity." Her grandmother pinched her lips together. "*Hmph.* I'd best see about updating my will at once."

"I don't understand." Sarah sat back on her heels and furrowed her forehead.

"I'm onto Bernice and Stinkwiggon's dastardly scheme now, the unscrupulous fiends," Grandmama muttered to herself, pounding the unfortunate armchair again.

Stinkwiggon? Surely she had misheard. "Stinkwiggon?"

Grandmother spared her a starchy glance. "Stinkwiggon's my fusty, calculating butler. He and Wattle think I don't know they've been dallying with one another for years. I may be old, but I'm neither blind nor stupid." She tapped the fingers of one arthritic hand upon the carved wood, her vexation palpable. Her small frame quaked with outrage

"It was your butler who turned us away," Sarah said. Grandmother must be made aware of the truth. God only knew what else her butler and companion were capable of.

Likely, the conniving butler had intercepted her letters, too. By returning Mama's correspondence, they made Mama believe her parents hadn't forgiven her. Things were starting to become quite clear.

"Yes, well," Grandmother huffed, her agitation turning her cheeks pink, "he'll be without a position as soon as I return home. So will Miss Bernice Wattle. She'll not find anyone willing to retain her in all of England. Neither will he, by God, by the time I'm done with them. Thought to pull the wool over my eyes, did they? Thought I was a dafty old tabby, did they? We'll see about that," she harrumphed.

Sarah almost felt sorry for the servants.

Almost.

She didn't doubt her grandmother's extensive influence, not to mention her far-reaching wrath, would prevent the pair from finding employment in London again. Or mayhap England, as she'd claimed.

"I've no doubt they've been intercepting letters intended for me with the intent of gaining an inheritance for themselves." Stuffing her handkerchief back into its hiding place, Grandmother pursed her mouth in displeasure.

"I think you must be right," Sarah agreed, her head slightly reeling with all she'd just learned.

Thanks to her devious servants, Grandmother had been as

much a victim as she and Chris. *Mama, too.* If Grandmother was right, Stinkwiggon and Miss Wattle deserved the consequences of their scurrilous actions.

Sarah rose, and after taking a seat in a nearby chair, pressed her lips together. "You should know that a very evil man is pursuing Chris and me. He killed our father, and we fled Jamaica, fearing for our lives."

Her almost invisible eyebrows skittering up her forehead, Grandmother whispered, "Dear God." She clasped Sarah's hand. "You poor, poor dear."

"Last week he found us, and if it hadn't been for Gregor McTavish's protection and kindheartedness, and that of several of the peeresses here today, as well as their husbands, Santano might've already abducted us." Or worse. "Mr. McTavish has devised a plan to entrap Santano, and hopefully, he will be arrested soon."

"My darling girl, you've had such a time of it. It seems I owe Mr. McTavish a debt of gratitude, too." She peered at Sarah, a trifle too keenly for her comfort. "May I presume he is that giant of a man who escorted you today?"

"Yes." Sarah tipped her head in acknowledgment. She wasn't quite ready for her grandmother to go poking around in that area when she didn't know exactly where she and Gregor stood with each other.

"Tell me…" Grandmother swallowed and patted another tear from the corner of her eye. "Does…" Her throat worked, and a tear dribbled down her papery cheek. "Does my Mary live?"

Sorrow engulfed Sarah. "I honestly do not know, Grandmama." How strange it felt on her tongue to address the woman as such. "I hope she does with all my heart."

"As do I."

Fighting her own tears, and struggling for composure,

Sarah glanced outside. "Why, it's snowing. I've never seen snow before."

Huge snowflakes fluttered from the sky, casting a fluffy white blanket on everything, even as she watched. Chris would be ecstatic.

"So it is." Grandmama turned her head. "It's been an unusually cold winter thus far. The trip home may be a bit of a challenge. We shouldn't delay overly long."

Did that mean she intended for Sarah to accompany her?

The dowager cleared her throat, drawing her attention. Trepidation shone in her grandmother's red-rimmed eyes. "Can you tell me what you do know?" Her gaze silently pleaded with Sarah.

"Mama was sickly when I left. She'd been frail for years. The tropical climate didn't agree with her all that well. When Santano commandeered Papa's ship, she made me take Chris and flee Jamaica. We scarcely had more than the clothes on our backs, but Mama and Papa had suspected Santano was up to something nefarious and had made arrangements for passage to England for us. She told me to contact you once we arrived three years ago. She sent a letter too." Hitching a shoulder, she dropped her gaze to her lap. "So, I don't know whether she lives or not."

Speaking those words out loud drove a dagger deep into her middle and twisted it. Sarah folded her hands, clasping her fingers tight, and crossed her ankles.

"Three years?" Agony etched the old woman's face. "Dear God. How have you and your brother managed to survive?"

"We had a few pieces of jewelry and some money." Sarah raised her chin. She would not be embarrassed, nor would she accept condemnation. "We've scraped by, living in unsavory neighborhoods you've probably never even ridden a carriage through."

Grandmama closed her eyes as if her shame were too great

to even look upon Sarah. "This, what you and your brother have endured, is my fault. I tried to force Mary to wed a man she didn't love. A man too old for her. She didn't care about his title or wealth. She wanted love. How she must have suffered, and you children, as well."

Sarah wouldn't deny it, not even to mollify her grandmother.

Mustering her composure, Grandmother offered a watery smile. "Well, if you'll permit me, my dear, I intend to make up for those years of neglect. You and Chris must come live with me. I have a rambling old house that has lacked laughter for far too long."

Relief washed over Sarah, as profound as if a lodestone had been lifted from her shoulders. Thank God Gregor had talked her into trying to contact her grandmother one more time. And thank God the Duchess of Harcourt had insisted on this tea party. For the first time in three years, she could actually anticipate Christmastide with a degree of joy.

"Thank you, Grandmother."

That trio of softly uttered words was all Sarah could achieve, so overcome with emotion, was she. This was what she'd hoped and prayed for, and now that the moment was upon her, she couldn't quite conceive it was happening.

Even as the thought crossed her mind, another more sobering one did, as well. What of her and Gregor? He meant to return to Scotland. Would she see him anymore?

You must, her heart cried. Even if that meant bolstering her courage and telling Gregor her feelings. Of her love. He felt something for her, too. Nothing could convince her otherwise.

What did she have to lose by doing so?

She and Chris might've found a home with their grandmother, but Sarah's heart had already found a home with a blond Highlander possessing a wicked smile and rakish twinkle in his eye.

"My Fifi—she's my Pomeranian—may be a mite jealous of you at first." A self-deprecating smile tipped Grandmama's thin lips. "I fear I've rather spoiled her. Loneliness will do that to a person."

"I'm sure we'll march on splendidly. I've always wanted a pet dog. Chris has too."

"Then you must have one," Grandma's voice brooked no dissent. "Both of you. *Hmm,*" she said, giving Sarah a speculative look. "We must find you a lady's maid, straightaway. It won't do for you to toddle about London unchaperoned, and I rarely attend functions these days. Though I might venture out a few times in the coming weeks to introduce you to Society."

"I have no need for a chaperone, Grandmama, or a maid, either." Her grandmother looked so disconcerted, Sarah softened her declaration with a smile. "I'm almost five-and-twenty, and I assure you, given where Chris and I have lived, and the hardships we've endured, I don't give a whit what anyone else thinks of my reputation. I know the truth, and that's what counts."

"Very well, my dear," Grandmother conceded. "But you'll need a maid to help you dress. Today's fashions cannot always be managed by one's self. You can determine when and if she accompanies you on outings. Is that agreeable?"

She appeared so eager to please, Sarah didn't have the heart to deny her. On the other hand, Grandmama wasn't going to dictate to her. She'd been independent too long. "That's acceptable. If I have a say in who is hired for the position."

"Of course." Grandmother's face brightened, and she clasped her hands to her breast. "Oh, what a Christmastide this shall be. I haven't celebrated since your mother left all those years ago. We used to make plum pudding together."

"Mama always made Christmas pudding."

A single tear made a track down Grandmama's face. "And gingerbread? How Mary adored gingerbread."

"And...gingerbread." Sarah pressed a palm to her mouth, fearing the dam of emotions she'd kept at bay, had refused to yield to, could no longer be held back.

"Come here, Sarah." Grandmother opened her arms.

At once, she knelt before her and burying her face in the crook of her grandmother's neck, smelling of lavender and roses, burst into tears.

"There, there, my dear." Grandmama made comforting sounds in her throat, all the while patting Sarah's back. "We have each other now."

At last, her tears spent, Sarah sat up and retrieved her own handkerchief. As she composed herself, a twinkle entered her Grandmama's eyes. "Tell me about that Scot you came with. I believe you have a fondness for him? Did I hear he's related to Viscount Sethwick?"

"He's Gregor McTavish, and Viscount Sethwick's his cousin." Lest her grandmother have any ideas about dictating who she spent time with, Sarah squared her shoulders. "I am more than fond of him. I love him."

Thirteen

Gregor sat across from Sarah as the carriage rumbled through Mayfair's elite streets. The sprinkling of snow four days ago had long since melted. Too bad, since he'd hoped to take her and Chris for an outing complete with hot drinking chocolate and roasted chestnuts. Had they been in Scotland, he'd teach her to ice skate.

Extremely fetching in a raspberry-toned redingote trimmed in black fur with a matching hat and muff, she'd been quiet and preoccupied most of the ride. Every now and again, her lips twitched the merest bit, and she sighed softly.

Would he ever tire of watching her?

Not in a lifetime.

He'd called to take her on the promised ride through Hyde Park today, and when she'd descended the stairs, uncustomary nervousness pummeled him. Given Lady Rolandson's caustic reputation, he'd expected the dowager to eviscerate him with her hostile gaze. Instead, she welcomed him warmly and hadn't even balked at their lack of chaperone.

No doubt Sarah could be credited there. His tropical

flower had turned out to be quite independent and strong-minded.

Permitting himself a thin, secret smile, he adjusted the cuff of his coat. He had something exceptional in store for Sarah. He only hoped he hadn't overstepped the mark. "Ye dinna look as happy as I thought ye would with the news that Santano and his crew were arrested."

Gregor was well pleased that his plan had gone off with nary a hitch.

Last night, Santano had broken into the warehouse, only to be confronted by him, a half dozen Bow Street Runners, as well as Ewan, Clarendon, Warrick, Ramsbury, and Harcourt.

"Those two ruffians we caught that night at the theater couldn't wait to turn against Santano." In the unlikely event, they were spared the hanging they deserved, for their testimony, the pair could expect to live the rest of their miserable lives in an Australian penal colony. "They provided enough information to have the mutinied crew members also arrested for murder, the Bow Street Runners informed me this morning."

Sarah brushed a hand over her thigh, her eyes more jade green than brown today. "I confess, I am profoundly relieved. Tonight, I shall sleep well for the first time in years." Her pretty bowed mouth tipped upward, and he yearned to taste those soft lips again. "I can never thank you enough, Gregor. And I'm very grateful for all that you've done, at great risk to yourself too."

Gratitude wasn't what he wanted from her. "Then what has ye lookin' so downtrodden, *leannan*?"

A sorrowful sigh escaped her, and she shifted on the seat. "This morning, my grandmother reminded me that we still don't know whether Mama lives." She palmed her tummy. "There's this persistent knot here, in my middle, that won't go away because I don't know." Her tongue darted out, moistening her lower lip. Throat convulsing, she turned her face away, obviously fighting tears.

Gregor couldn't bear her suffering and crossed the carriage to sit beside her. He gathered her into his embrace, and she immediately turned her face into his chest, wrapped her arms about his torso, and wept.

"*Shh, leannan, mo ghoal.*" Calling her, *my love* wasn't so very bold, considering Sarah didn't speak Gaelic. He ran a hand up and down her spine, admiring the gently sloping curve even as he comforted her.

"Oh, Gregor." His greatcoat muffled her voice. "What would I do without you?"

"Dinna give up hope." He laid his cheek atop her head. "If I recall correctly, Captain Piermont is scheduled to sail to the Caribbean soon. I've already asked him to check on your mother." If all went as he intended, he'd be by Sarah's side for the rest of his life, and she'd never have to fend for herself again.

She tilted her face, her eyelashes adorably spiky, and her cheeks rosy from her cry. "I'll write a letter to send with the captain, too. So that Mama knows Captain Piermont is trustworthy."

Resisting her slightly parted rosebud lips proved as futile as denying his growing homesickness for Scotland. Lifting her onto his lap, he cradled her in his arms and tasted her luscious mouth.

Sarah sighed again, only this was the sound of a contented woman. Twining her arms about his neck, she urged him closer. She opened her mouth to his tongue's gentle probing, and he deepened the kiss.

Desire, lust, and profound longing tunneled through his veins, filling every pore, and swelling within his heart. This woman had become something so precious in such a short time, he must convince her to marry him.

He *would* convince her.

After several more delicious minutes of exploring her mouth, he finally raised his head. The carriage had left the central part of London and bounced along a less busy lane on the town's outskirts. Good thing too, for his rash impulse wouldn't have served her reputation well had they been seen.

Cuddling her in his arms, he dropped a kiss atop her bonneted head.

The carriage hit a bump, and Sarah came down hard on Gregor's lap. At once, hot, intense desire flooded his groin. Gritting his teeth against the sweet torture, he shifted her onto the seat once more, then wiped away her tears with his thumbs.

His hair had come loose during their kiss, and she grasped a handful.

"I like that you haven't cut your hair. It suits the rugged Scotsman that you are far better than the Titus or Brutus." She giggled, holding a few tendrils out to the side and jiggling them up and down. "Or heaven forbid, the frightened owl."

Rotating a finger near his head, he chuckled. "Can ye imagine all of this styled in the frightened owl fashion?"

She dropped her focus to his fancy togs. "You might dress the perfect English gentleman, but at heart, you're Scot through and through, Gregor." Head to the side, she considered him. "I don't believe managing Stapleton Shipping and Supplies is what you're meant to do, no matter how good you might be at the position."

Neither did he.

"I think you should pursue becoming a doctor," she announced.

Edinburgh did have an outstanding medical school.

Sarah had grown up on a tropical island, and more than once expressed how much she disliked England's drizzly, gray clime. Could he convince her to make Scotland, with its harsher weather, craggy terrain, and rugged people her home?

There'd be plenty of time to consider that later.

He'd reinforce his efforts to court her, and his surprise today was sure to earn him a place in her heart.

Rather than return to the opposite seat, he tucked her close to his side and took her hand in his. Yuletide was less than a week away, but he couldn't wait that long to give her the gift he'd found for her.

They traveled in silence for several minutes, and when he glanced down, it was to discover she'd fallen asleep, her head nestled against his shoulder.

She hadn't been sleeping well, fretting for her brother and herself. Now that her grandmother had acknowledged her, Sarah's life would be so much easier. Her mother was the final thing that plagued her peace.

Hopefully, Piermont would return with good news in the spring.

Stretching his legs out before him, Gregor rested his head against the squabs. He had more to overcome than Sarah's dislike of the climate. Her grandmother was a wealthy, powerful woman, and if he convinced her to marry him, though they'd never go without necessities, he wasn't in a position to shower fine things upon her.

He opened his eyes and touched his lips to the top of her bonnet. Nae, Sarah cared more about character and what was in a person's heart than being draped in fine silk and glittering jewels.

A few more minutes passed before the carriage juddered to a stop.

"Sarah?" Gregor gently shook her shoulders. "Sarah, wake up, lass. I've another surprise for ye. It's an early Yuletide present from me."

Blinking drowsily, she raised her sleepy gaze to his, and the tenderness there humbled him. Still sleep-drugged, her irises were a haunting shade somewhere between blue and green with gold flecks today. He loved that about her. Her eyes changed color depending on what she wore or her current mood.

"Another surprise? What have you done now, Highlander?" Excitement twinkled in the depths of her gaze, and she cast an inquisitive glance out the window. "Where are we?"

"You'll have to wait and see, *jo*." He gave her a seductive wink.

The carriage door swung open, and the driver lowered the steps.

Gregor descended first, then extended his hand to assist her from the carriage.

Her face awash with curiosity, she inspected the stately manor on London's perimeter.

After some lengthy inquiries, he had finally found what he sought. For a time, he feared the task he'd set himself impossible to complete, but with the help of Ramsbury, Harcourt, and Ewan, he'd met with success.

"Why are we here?" Sarah took in her surroundings. "Am I meeting yet another titled relative?"

"Nae." Gregor lifted the knocker, and almost at once, a cheerful maid opened the door.

A secret in her eyes, she bobbed a curtsy. "Mr. Stallworth is expecting you, sir."

Sarah preceded him into the house and glanced around, her forehead furrowed with two neat rows.

"This way, please, Mr. McTavish, miss." The maid indicated they should follow her.

Completely bewildered, Sarah asked, "Gregor, whatever are you about?"

"You'll just have to wait and see." Unfamiliar giddiness

bubbled behind his ribs. He couldn't remember ever going to such efforts for a present before. And this would be the first Christmas gift he'd ever given.

True, he was giving it to Sarah early, but nonetheless...

The maid led them toward the back of the house, down a long corridor, then to a cozy room off the kitchen. A man rose from beside a short, wooden enclosure, and smiling, extended his hand.

"Mr. McTavish. It's a pleasure to see you again. I see you've brought the young lady you told me about."

"Sarah, this is Able Stallsworth," Gregor said. "Mr. Stallsworth, Miss Sarah Paine."

Squeaking and rustling from the enclosure hinted at Gregor's surprise.

Eyes going round in excitement and astonishment, her mouth formed a perfect little "o." She rushed to the box, and giggling, sank to her knees. "Oh, Gregor. Nothing could be more perfect." She scooped a wriggling black dachshund pup into each hand and held them against her cheeks. Cooing softly, she kissed their shiny heads. "Aren't you the most precious darlings?"

"Happy Christmas, Sarah," Gregor said, his throat oddly tight with sentiment.

She turned such a look of utter adoration on him, he didn't doubt she was meant to be his for all time. Everything that had happened that had brought them to this point had been part of a grand plan. She was his destiny as surely as snow was cold and fire burned hot.

Stallsworth gave a deferential half bow.

"You have your pick of the litter, Miss Paine. No one else has claimed a pup yet. It will be another two weeks before they are ready to leave their mother, however. Let me know which one you want, and I'll tie a ribbon around its neck. I'll give you a few minutes alone with them." At the door, he turned back. "By the by, their mother's name is Elsa."

Such joy radiated from Sarah's face, Gregor could have watched her for hours.

Such a simple thing—the gift of a pup—and she reacted as if he'd presented her with a chest of jewels. Although, knowing her as he did, she preferred heartfelt gestures to gems and valuable trinkets.

She cast him an uncertain look then sucked her lower lip between her teeth. "Gregor?"

He joined her on the floor, accepting a pup to cuddle. The little devil promptly bit his nose. "Aye, lass?"

"There are only three, and I know Chris would also love to have one. I cannot bear to think that a puppy will be left behind." Uncertainty made her hesitant. "May I... I know it's a lot to ask... And of course, Grandmother would have to be agreeable, as well as Mr. Stallworth. But might-I-be-permitted-*all*-of-them?" she finished in a rush of words.

Gregor bent and kissed each cheek, then boldly pressed his mouth to hers. "One for each Christmas ye've missed? Aye, that seems fair."

He laid his pup in his lap and lifted her hand to his lips. "I have a request of ye, too, my tropical flower."

"Yes?" Eyes shining, she cocked her head as she returned the three puppies to their worried mother.

"Will ye marry me, *mo ghaol*? I dinna ken where I'll be in a year, but I plan on applyin' to medical school in Scotland. We'll have to live at Craiglocky in the meanwhile, and I ken ye're no' used to the severe clime there. It will also mean leavin' yer grandmother, and ye've only just begun to ken her—"

"Do shush, Gregor."

He searched her face. "Is it too soon? I can give ye more time to get to ken me better."

"None of that other matters, silly man." She laid a palm against his cheek. "Since the day I barged into your office, and you helped me without hesitation, I knew there was something special about you. With each passing day, my heart grew fuller, and though I kept telling myself it was impossible to already love you, my spirit said otherwise. I would follow you to the ends of the earth, Gregor McTavish."

He crushed her to his chest, laughing. "Thank God. I feared it was too soon. I love ye, Sarah. So much it frightens me as nothing ever has before."

"And I love you. I'll always remember this Yuletide as the one when a Highlander stole my heart." She smiled and whispered against his mouth. "Now, kiss me."

Epilogue

Suttford House, Scottish Highlands

June 21, 1826

Sarah awoke slowly, rousing from a deep, comfortable slumber. Drowsily patting the mattress beside her, she came fully awake. Though warmth met her palm, Gregor's familiar form did not. She sat up, pushing the hair off her face and shivered. The fire burned low in the hearth, and the wind buffeting the windows revealed the winter storm that had threatened yesterday was fully upon them now.

Out of habit, she searched the chamber for him. He was wont to rise at all manner of hours over the past four years to study or take down a note for one reason or another. The room was empty, save the three lumps buried in their bed beside the wardrobe. Baron, Dickens, and Fergie slept on, oblivious to the storm buffeting the house.

In the end, Chris had confessed he preferred cats to dogs, and that's how Cat came to live with the Dowager Viscountess Rolandson. He'd grown impossibly more spoiled and pampered, which put him in good company with Fifi and the dachshunds.

Sarah grasped the coverlet, prepared to pull it aside when the bedchamber door swung open.

Gregor, attired only in his trousers and shirt, slipped inside, cradling their fretting five-month-old son, Bryce. He closed the panel and pressed a kiss to his son's head. "The wee bairn thinks he's starvin'."

Though unfashionable, she'd elected to nurse her babe as she had Aaron, his almost two-year-old brother. Extending her arm, she gave a slight shake of her head and accepted her son's sturdy little body. She sank into the pile of pillows, and after unlacing the front of her gown, set Bryce to her breast. Bending, she kissed his satiny cheek and inhaled his sweet scent.

"How could I have not heard him?" she asked.

"He didna cry verra long. I only heard him because I was awake, thinkin' about the school and hospital." He chuckled and shook his head. "Yer mother and grandmother were already fussin' over him by the time I arrived. They changed his flannels too."

"I'm not surprised. They both adore helping." She raised an eyebrow and pushed her lower lip out a jot. "Why were you awake? Dr. McTavish, don't tell me you're nervous?"

"No' nervous, *mo ghaol*."

Thanks to the generosity of his family and other wealthy peers' patronage, the dream she and Gregor had shared years ago to build an orphanage, a school, and a hospital for the physically incapacitated had become a reality.

New Hope Institution would officially open on January first, but seven-and-twenty children already occupied the hundred-bed orphanage, and the school had a waiting list, as well. Chris would continue to live with Mama at Grandmother's but attend the school during the day.

After adding coal to the fire, Gregor shucked his shirt and trousers, and bare as the day he was born, climbed into the bed beside her. He, too, propped himself against the pillows before tugging her against the hard planes of his slightly hairy chest and dropping a kiss onto her forehead.

"Even after all this time, Gregor, whenever I see that scar on your side, my stomach twists sickeningly. To think, I might have lost you before I even found you."

"It disna even pain me anymore," he assured her.

Inserting his forefinger into Bryce's tiny fist, the babe's fingers hardly encircling half Gregor's pickle-sized digit, he chuckled as their son suckled voraciously. "He has an appetite like his brother."

Sarah looked above her and ran a hand over Gregor's bristly jaw. "Our sons have appetites like their father and Uncle Alasdair."

He chuckled, grazing her temple with his mouth. "Aye, they do. All the McTavish men eat like they're hollow to their feet."

Bryce's hazel-blue gaze shifted between Sarah and Gregor, and he grinned. A droplet of milk trailed from his mouth before he resumed his eager feasting.

Gregor brushed his fingertips up and down her arm. Even through her night rail's light fabric, the caress sent sensuous chills to more interesting places.

"Why weren't you sleeping at," she glanced at the bedside clock, "two in the morning, if you weren't worrying?

His boyish grin held a hint of bashfulness. "I'm already plannin' the second facility that Yvette is sponsorin' in Scotland. What do ye think about namin' it Second Hope Institution?"

"That's perfect, Gregor." She sighed and settled into his chest a bit deeper. "I knew there was a need, but I hadn't expected the overwhelming response we've seen. It makes me sad we can't do more."

"Och, we'll do what we can, and continue to advocate and ask others to." He turned his attention to their son still contentedly nursing. "Between yer mother and grandmother and my mother, I fear all our bairns will be spoiled."

"Not a bit of it. I don't believe a child can ever be loved too much." With her bent forefinger, she brushed the babe's cheek. "I can scarce fathom that Mama's been back in England almost as long as Chris and I were here without her. I'm so grateful because I feared Grandmother would be horribly lonely when we married and returned to Scotland."

"Aye, and glad I am our bairns will ken her," Gregor whispered as he gently extracted his finger. "Our wee son's asleep, *jo.*"

His little mouth slack, Bryce had succumbed to slumber once more.

A soft rap announced Mama had come to take her grandson back to the nursery. This had become a routine in recent weeks, while Sarah and Gregor stayed at Grandmama's until the finishing touches on New Hope were complete.

Two infants, four dogs, a pompous cat, and a mischievous parrot—yes, Biscuit had made the ocean voyage too—could be quite chaotic at times. Initially, Sarah and Gregor had planned on letting a house, but Grandmama wouldn't have it. She insisted all were welcome to stay with her and said a little excitement would do her good.

In fact, she thrived on the commotion and nearing her five-and-seventieth birthday, claimed to be healthier than she had been in decades. No longer having a broken heart or treacherous servants likely had much to do with her renewed vigor.

The last they'd heard, Miss Wattle and Stinkwiggon had

boarded a ship for America. Grandmother's hand didn't reach that far. Yet.

Sarah couldn't deny Mama and Grandmama's help with an energetic toddler, and an infant was most welcome.

"Here, let me have the laddie." Gregor accepted the small bundle, the same expression of awe on his face she'd observed every time he gazed at his children. That this brawny Highlander who dwarfed so many other men became a gentle giant with their sons made her eyes misty.

After they'd wed, he'd confessed he hadn't thought to ever marry and have children. She'd never deny the path to their meeting had been a long, treacherous hard-won journey, but that made their love all the more wondrous.

Once Sarah secured the front of her gown, she slipped from the bed. Cuddling Bryce in the crook of her arm, she padded barefoot to the door. A quick glance over her shoulder assured her Gregor had pulled the bedcoverings to his chin, sparing Mama any blushes. Still, his naughty wink and suggestive smile sent Sarah's pulse skittering.

She opened the door, and as she expected, her mother waited there. Taking her grandson into her arms, a doting smile curving her mouth, she murmured, "I see a bit of your father's nose and jawline."

Mama still grieved Papa's death.

"I do too." Sarah kissed her son's smooth forehead, inhaling a deep breath. Nothing smelled as wonderful as her children, except for perhaps, the brawny Scot waiting in bed. She hadn't missed the hunger in his eyes, but he could be patient a little longer.

Sarah bussed her mother's cheek, admonishing gently, "Don't stay up too long, Mama. You also need your sleep."

"Tish tosh." Mama shook her head. "I have years to sleep. This sweet one will only be little for a short time."

Leaning against the doorframe, Sarah watched as her mother, humming softly, wandered toward the nursery.

Overjoyed didn't begin to describe her emotion when the letter from Mama had arrived at Craiglocky Keep saying she was safe and well at Grandmama's house, along with Biscuit. When Santano had raided Bellewood, she and Ionie, their Jamaican housekeeper and cook, had huddled in the hidden chamber. Knowing he would likely return, Mama had secretly gone to live with Ionie in her village, taking the chamber's contents and burying the valuables.

Under the care of the village healer, Mama's health had gradually improved. Weekly, a nephew of Ionie's discreetly inquired at the harbor, seeking news of Sarah or Santano. That was how Mama learned of Piermont's arrival and Sarah's letter. She'd tried to talk Ionie into coming with her to England, but the servant wouldn't leave her family.

Chris would never have to worry about his future. The *Mary Elizabeth* had been sold to Stapleton Shipping and Supplies, and the proceeds from the sale of Bellewood House had been invested on Christopher's behalf. As she'd suspected, the chest contained unimaginable treasure. Treasure, Mama adamantly maintained, Papa received for saving a privateer's life many years before. She would speak no more on the subject, giving Sarah cause to speculate there might've been other less honorable reasons they'd always lived in Jamaica.

Before climbing back in bed, she wandered to the window and pulled the drapery aside. "You're right, Gregor. There's quite a snowstorm outside."

When he didn't respond, she glanced at the bed.

He ran his appreciative gaze down her form, and she realized the firelight gave him a perfect view of her body silhouetted in the flowing gown. A more carnal visage replaced his admiration, and his facial features stood out sharply hewn, in what she'd come to recognize as desire.

Giving him a sultry smile, she unlaced her gown, slipped it off her shoulders, and wiggled free of its folds, allowing it to pool at her feet.

Inhaling a rasping breath, he opened his arms wide. "Come here, *leannan*."

She ran to the bed and threw herself into his waiting arms.

With a half-growl half-groan, in one deft movement, Gregor rolled her beneath him and entered her. All he ever had to do was glance at her with seduction in his gaze, and she was ready to receive him.

As he rose above her, passion sharpening his features, she wrapped her arms around his broad back and arched into his hips.

"I love you, my brawny Highlander."

"And I ye, my precious tropical flower."

~

I hope you enjoyed
A YULETIDE HIGHLANDER
If you'd like to leave a review, I would be grateful.

Keep reading for a free preview of
TO LOVE A HIGHLAND LAIRD
Book 1
Heart of a Scot Series...

~

TO LOVE A HIGHLAND LAIRD
Heart of a Scot
Book 1

Outside Glenliesh Village,
Near Dunrangour Tower

12 March 1720

Mayra grinned at the days-old dun calves frolicking in the meadow, gleaming as if blanketed with enormous emeralds. Early-blooming Lady's Smock added faint lilac patches here and there. And if she weren't mistaken, a few bluebells already bobbed their cheerful heads amongst the green bordering the Windlespoons' estate.

The cold, wet winter seemed to drag on, each day longer than the previous. But at last, spring was almost upon the Highlands, and several shrubs and trees blossomed prematurely.

She wouldn't stop and say hello to her dearest friend, Gaira, today. Gaira's doting parents had whisked her to Edinburgh for the Social Season, something Mayra would never experience.

Envy tried to jab her, but she resolutely tamped the dark sentiment down and focused on the lovely day instead.

As she expertly guided the dog cart along the muddy, rutted path still dotted with puddles from last night's blustery showers, Mayra smiled for the sheer joy of the sun's stroking rays and the vivid azure sky peeping between the ever-present silver-tinted clouds.

These were the days when she relished the Highlands; when spring promised new life, fresh hope, and possibly even a wee romping adventure.

Och, so wonderful, if only it might be so.

She detested the rain—almost a treasonous attitude for a Scot.

Yet the dampness, as well as everything cloaked in ugly grayish hues from palest ash to deepest charcoal—day after day, weeks on end—wore on her.

Especially since her only regular reprieve from the keep—also pewter-colored from its corbelling and crow-stepped gables to its corner turrets and bartizans—were these twice-weekly visits to the village.

Always—*always, God's teeth*—accompanied by someone.

Usually a clan member, one or two of her rapscallion teenage brothers, or Mayra's diligent middling-aged maid, Bettie. On rare occasions, dear Mum joined Mayra, but since Da had died two years ago, those instances had grown fewer and fewer.

The latter pairs' keen regard seldom left her longer than a minute, so seriously did they take her chaperonage. Consequently, nothing the least bit exciting ever occurred on the jaunts. Unless Mayra counted her brothers' penchant for regularly becoming embroiled in mischief of some sort in the village.

Today, Bettie sat in the dog cart's rear seat, food baskets for the needy tucked inside the rectangular box beneath her. She snored softly as Mayra skillfully guided Horace, their mild-tempered, going-to-fat gelding, along the well-worn, rutted path passing for a road.

No need to rush the horse. She'd delay her return as long as possible.

"I promised Maggi MacPherson I'd stop in for a short visit and share a pot of tea today after I deliver the baskets."

Mayra spared a swift glance behind her.

Chin drooping, Bettie dozed, her cream kerchief-covered head bouncing with each jar of the cart.

"Bettie?"

She stirred and blinked sleepily while yawning behind her hand.

"Do ye want to go with me, Bettie? Or would ye rather take a cup with yer sister, and I can collect ye afterward?"

"I'd like to see ye to the inn and then walk to Agnes', but I'm feelin' a wee bit waff." She sneezed and blinked watery eyes. "If ye promise no' to be more than a half an hour, Mayra, I suppose ye can see yerself there this one time. Straight to The Dozin' Stag and back, ye hear? Nae dawdlin' or givin' anyone cause to wag their tongue."

Did anyone ever need cause to blether?

Not in Mayra's limited experience.

"I dinna dawdle, as ye well ken. Besides, I canna imagine what could occur in such a short time that would raise even a single eyebrow hair."

Nothing exciting ever happened to Mayra. Ever.

"*Hmph.*" Bettie made a mollified sound before sneezing again. Her plum-round cheeks slightly flushed, she pulled her shawl snugger. "And let's be keepin' it that way, shall we?"

Arching an indignant brow, Mayra directed her attention back to the road as the neat village loomed ahead. Honestly, a little tittle-tattle on her behalf might prove most invigorating, given her wholly predictable and dull-as-a-worn-quill's life.

However, Bettie did appear a trifle peaked. Rather wan about her mouth too.

Swallowing her disappointment, Mayra released a slow sigh.

No loitering in the village today.

After she made her excuses to Maggi, she'd see Bettie home and to her bed as quickly as possible. She'd take no chances with her beloved servant's health.

An hour later, having delivered food baskets to Widow Ainsley, the kind but dotty Pinkerton sisters, Dunrangour's deaf-as-a-turnip retired gardener, and four more to the kirk for other villagers in need, she drew the equipage before the MacPhersons' charming three-story lodging house.

Nearly a century of weather had worn the stone surface to a welcoming mellow, tawny-slate, a delightful contrast to the faded paint-chipped, poppy-red shutters.

As always, mouth-watering smells wafted from within, and Mayra's stomach gurgled in anticipation of enjoying one of Maggi MacPherson's Scotch pies. Mayra had skipped breakfast, and now she'd have to bear a hollow middle until she returned home.

Pressing a hand against her rumbling tummy, she squared her shoulders. More than one unfortunate villager dealt with hunger daily these past months. Assuredly, she could endure another hour or so.

"G'day, Miss Findlay."

A ready grin split Reed MacPherson's winter-pale face when Horace nudged his chest, demanding the boy rub his withers.

As the lad reached for the reins before obliging the persistent horse, she smiled.

Standing on his toes, Reed scratched Horace's coat just below his mane. "Ho, Horace. Ye like that, do ye?" Reed patted the gelding's side. "He's gettin' fatter, miss."

"Indeed, he is. Which is why it takes me so long to make the journey, though it's barely three miles. He's a lazy laddie, he is." She adjusted her *bergère* hat—sadly in need of a fresh ribbon—to a slightly jauntier angle. But how could she justify a new embellishment when villagers went without necessities? "I'll only be a few moments, Reed—just long enough to give yer mum my apologies. My abigail ails, and I must see her swiftly home."

"Aye, miss. I'll keep him company for ye. Saved him a carrot too."

Horace—his eyes half-closed in contentment—blew out a shuddery breath and bent his right leg. He'd not be pleased at having to turn right around and head for home. Too much exertion for one morning for the old boy.

"Ye spoil him, Reed."

Giving a soft laugh, Mayra stood. After pulling her wide skirt to the side, she prepared to descend the cart, a task she usually managed well without assistance, despite wearing panniers.

Searc MacPherson exited the inn with a man she'd never seen before. Hands behind his back and broad neck bent, Searc shook his head slowly at something the striking man said.

Just then, the stranger glanced upward and his arresting hazel eyes tangled with hers, jarring Mayra to her toes. And then he smiled—a dazzling flash of teeth in his tanned face.

In a twinkling, her mind went as blank as a sheet of fresh foolscap.

In a completely foreign fashion, she became all gangly

limbs, caught her toe on her hem, and with a strangled squawk—somewhere between a crane's whoop and a sheep's bleat—toppled right off the cart.

Into his arms.

Oh, curdled custard.

Leaping forward, he'd somehow managed to close the distance in the blink of an eye. The alternative, being splayed on the ground in a wholly unladylike fashion, possibly injured, didn't bear contemplating.

She found herself clasped to a marvelous, solidly muscled chest while equally impressive firm arms cradled her shoulders and legs. The barest hint of mahogany whiskers shadowed the angular breadth of his neck and jaw—mere delicious inches away—and she forgot to breathe.

What a magnificent specimen of manhood. And he held her in his arms. Hopefully, he'd never let go.

Quite the most spectacular, fortunate accident ever to befall a maiden.

When her faulty lungs decided to function again, the most pleasant masculine scent filled her nostrils. Not a heavy fragrance, but a fresh, crisp, yet slightly musky scent—perhaps a hint of ale and tobacco too.

She inhaled a thorough, prolonged breath. Probably indecorous, that, although neither Mum nor Bettie had ever specifically warned her against sniffing gentlemen amid their other rigid advice.

Who was he?

Why hadn't she seen him in Glenliesh before?

Perhaps he only traveled through their unremarkable hamlet?

Och, of course he did. The small village offered little in the way of entertainment or commerce.

Why did the thought cause such profound disappointment?

Mayra wasn't free to harbor romantic notions; not even in the most secret, most remote recesses of her mind. Well, fine, perhaps in the most clandestine, most isolated niches that even she daren't peek at except once or twice.

In the dark of night.

With her head buried beneath her thick coverlet.

From the *cuaran* boots enclosing the gentleman's feet to his nutmeg-colored jacket and dark blue waistcoat, the stranger's attire shouted quality. Hatless and tartan-free as he was, she couldn't hazard a guess as to his clan, or if he even boasted Scottish heritage at all.

Might he be a *Sassenach*?

A Frenchman?

Perhaps, but his vivid coloring implied Scots or Irish.

He cocked his russet head and his eyes, an unusual but enthralling shade between summer moss and toasted almonds, glinted merrily at her. An unhurried smile bent his strong lips, revealing a charming dimple in his left cheek and further crimping the corner of his twinkling eyes. From the creases also framing his strong, still upturned mouth, it appeared he smiled habitually.

Instead of mortification engulfing her—as would be appropriate—of its own accord, her mouth swept upward, accompanied by a wave of sheer and wholly foreign giddiness.

And by rumbledethumps, she, Mayra Effie Lilias Findlay, was not the giddy, gay, flibbertigibbet sort.

She didn't flirt or bat her eyes, or send secret messages to handsome gentlemen with her fan or gloves as Gaira was wont to do.

Perfectly content, Mayra made no effort to leave the blissful security of his arms, and he seemed disinclined to release her as well. And at five feet eight inches, she wasn't a wee sprite of a lass either. Yet his arms didn't tremble or shake with the exertion. In fact, she might've been a child, so effort-lessly did he hold her.

Rather made her feel dainty and feminine.

And ever so naughty.

She peeked over his wide, sturdy shoulder.

Och and rot.

Bettie—Mum, as well—would cluck and fuss something awful when they learned a man had held her—in public too.

They would know soon enough, since a few villagers had seen her ungraceful tumble, and even now stood gawking at the attractive stranger in their midst.

The young ladies in particular seemed enthralled. They stared brazenly while striking provocative poses and thrusting their bosoms out, the whole while tittering about the *"braw mon"* with the wavy auburn hair.

How could Mayra blame them, when even though each scandalous moment she lingered in the *"braw mon's"* embrace heaped scoops of coal on the gossip fires, she couldn't bring herself to move an inch?

It wasn't every day a lass found herself in such a wonder-fully awkward predicament.

Still, she ought to make some effort to leave his embrace.

Perhaps she'd contracted Bettie's ailment and fever had addled her reason.

Mayra touched her cheek, aware his startling, amused, greenish gaze trailed the movement.

Aye, verra warm.

That explained the languid heat encompassing her. Like warm honey trickled through her veins and turned her muscles to the consistency of hot-off-the-stove porridge.

And inarguably, no one had ever witnessed either warm honey or fresh porridge ever standing upright.

Finally clicking his gaping mouth closed, Searc trundled to her, his apron strings flapping against his ample behind.

"Lass, I feared ye were about to take a nasty fall." He slapped the other man on his broad shoulder. "Good thing, our friend here is quicker on his feet than I am, aye?"

"Indeed. I'm most grateful." Must she sound so dafty and breathless? "Ye may put me down now, sir."

Or not.

I dinna mind stayin' in yer arms a trifle longer.

A week or so perhaps

As if he'd heard her, the handsome stranger's grasp firmed, pulling her minutely closer, his fingers pressing into the undersides of her thighs in a most thrilling way. A way that made her yearn to nestle closer, nuzzle his strong, delicious-smelling neck, and press her backside into his palms.

Another heady wave sluiced through her.

Was it her imagination, or did he seem almost as reluctant to release her as she was to have him set her down?

After he lowered her to the ground, one of his hands lingered between her shoulder blades for a scrumptious, protracted moment. The heat penetrated her clothing, and she wouldn't be surprised when she disrobed tonight to find his palm imprinted on her back as if branded by his touch.

The urge to lean into his chest so overwhelmed her that she bit her lip.

What in Highland heather had come over her?

She'd been too shielded from young, devilishly attractive men, that was what. Other than family members, no male had ever embraced her. Good thing, too, if this was her doaty reaction.

Except...

Mayra doubted she'd respond like this with just any man.

A flush singed her already heated cheeks, and she set about righting her rumpled gown and lopsided hat, taking care to avoid the curious glances of the passersby. She must be above reproach, she well knew. Hadn't that been drilled into her over and over *and over* from the time she was a wee lass?

Aye, and Mayra always did what was expected of her.

Nonetheless, mightn't a scandal be just the thing to put her betrothed off?

Would her intended then *finally* grant her request to end their arrangement?

Perhaps.

As the idea took root, she paused with her fussing.

Aye, an innocent flirtation *was* just the thing.

Och, and when word reached—

"May I ken whom I've had the pleasure of rescuin'?" Her hero raked a big hand through his gingerish locks, ruffling the curls atop his head.

Och. Bless Mayra's darned and mended stockings, Scots after all.

The way he said pleasure, the word rolling from his tongue in a low, mesmerizing brogue-turned-purr, wrenched her attention from her ministrations to his much-too-enticing lips.

Since when did a man's mouth fascinate her so?

That same mouth notched up a trifle before her gaze inched higher to lock with his.

Her heart frolicked about behind her ribs like a litter of frisky kittens.

God help me.

A flirtation with this man might prove much too danger-ous. Given her uncharacteristic, dazed response, *he* might be much too dangerous.

"Allow me to introduce ye." Searc beamed, his wide face wreathed in an enormous smile. "Miss Mayra Findlay, may I present Mr.—"

Searc scratched the back of his bulging neck, his face

folded into confused creases. "I dinna recollect if I heard yer name when Mags registered ye."

Her hero dragged his attention from Mayra for an instant. "Och, aye...I'm...Coburn. Coburn Wallace."

As Mr. Wallace respectfully dipped his head, polite but not the least subservient, the sun caught the bronze streaks ribboning his russet hair.

"Mr. Coburn Wallace, Miss Mayra Findlay," Searc finished, another broad smile stretching his kind face, as if he'd been granted the highest honor in introducing them.

Mayra adjusted her sleeve, smoothing the slightly frayed cuff over her glove.

Och. No' done.

Searc only meant to be helpful, but in introducing her to the stranger, he overstepped propriety. Mum and Bettie wouldn't be pleased.

Mayra ought to nod her head and sweep past the men without another word. Most peculiar thing, however. Her feet stayed fixed where Mr. Wallace had deposited her and seemed as loath to move as Glen Coe's majestic mountains towering beyond the horizon.

"Miss Findlay? Of Dunrangour Tower?"

A different glint, keener and assessing rather than appreciative, entered Mr. Wallace's interesting eyes. His hot gaze leisurely crept to her scuffed half-boot clad feet and then made the reverse journey over her well-worn midnight-blue and hunter-green arisaid to rest on her hair secured in a simple knot beneath her hat.

"Aye, I am." Mayra's stomach renewed its frolicking when he'd said her name. Mindful of the intrigued onlookers, she inclined her head in what she hoped was a regal yet impersonal manner.

"May I ask what brings ye to our fair village, Mr. Wallace?"

~

DAMN HIS EYES, Logan was in it to his raised brows now. And he detested trickery.

"I'm visitin' relatives after three years abroad, Miss Findlay."

Not exactly a lie, but enough of a deception that his conscience chafed worse than sliding across Loch Tolhorf's frozen surface.

Bare arsed.

More precisely, he'd left Lockelieth in outrage after falling out with his father upon learning Da had spent a great deal— *nearly all, truth be told*—of Miss Findlay's dowry entrusted to his care until she and Logan wed.

Blinded by his much younger wife's exotic beauty, Da had succumbed to Rodena's extravagant demands. In doing so, he'd forsworn his scruples, violated the settlement terms, and obligated Logan to honor the cursed troth.

Unless he paid back the monies. Monies he didn't possess.

That had spurred him to delve into a variety of risky business ventures while abroad, a few teetering on respectability's fringes, and none of which paid a quick return.

But then again, he'd believed he had at least another year to make his fortune before exchanging vows.

Only—*blast my damnable luck*—two months ago, he'd received word his father had fallen gravely ill. On the harried journey home, time and again Logan cursed himself for losing his temper and departing without telling Da farewell.

He'd arrived home mere days before his father died, leaving Logan an undisciplined clan, nigh on destitute serfs, a keep in deplorable condition, and empty estate coffers. Not to mention a widow more distraught about her future than her husband's death or the care of her young daughter, Isla.

For a fortnight after Da's death, Logan had prowled

Lockelieth, half-pished in a grief-born fog, and later, a fury-born haze when he learned *all* of Mayra's dowry was now gone—squandered down to the last glistening pearl...on Rodena.

And that wasn't the worst hell-fired news.

Da had secretly mortgaged Lockelieth to her glorious ramparts and parapets with an impossibly large payment due by year's end.

A payment Logan had no means of making.

At present, Mayra's lands—lands Da claimed contained valuable ores—and the rest of her dowry were all that stood between Lockelieth and financial ruin.

More importantly, and the compelling reason he couldn't cancel the union with Mayra Findlay, Logan's people had suffered neglect these past few years as Da poured all his resources into Rodena's grasping, talon-tipped fingers.

Several clansmen murmured of dissent and rebellion so disillusioned were they by the plight Father had brought upon them.

Logan's foreign business ventures had yet to produce a significant profit, and his only recourse was to convince Mayra to marry him before her twentieth birthday.

Much sooner, truth to tell.

Ideally, as quickly as arrangements could be made.

No legal writ forbade him from wedding her sooner, just a reluctant six-year-old lad's oath of honor.

He eyed her, chatting with the lad petting her well-fed horse. She was as likely to agree to the rushed union as sheep were to frolic about wearing periwigs, sniffing snuff, and sipping sherry.

"Are ye from near here, Mr. Wallace?"

Mayra picked a piece of straw from her plaid. Her endearing, not so subtle attempt to glean more information earned her an amused smile.

He'd piqued her interest.

Excellent.

Logan could almost see and hear her mind ticking off possibilities.

"I have family scattered hither and yon in Scotland and England. Even a few in the New World, Miss Findlay."

True enough.

Unlike the falsehood he'd told her about his identity.

The lie spilled from his mouth before he could consider another wiser, more honest option.

Coburn wouldn't be pleased when he learned of the ruse, and even less so when Logan asked him to keep his confidence regarding the matter. Despite his reputation with the ladies, Coburn's integrity made even the most devout saint appear a black-hearted sinner.

Nevertheless, and despite Logan's lie relegating him to the worst sort of knave, he didn't want Mayra to know he was her affianced just yet. Particularly since a stack of letters requesting an end to their betrothal sat neatly within in his desk's top drawer—an ever-present reminder of her disdain and reluctance.

That was one reason he'd chosen to stay in the village for the time being, rather than venture to Dunrangour Tower directly. He was well within his rights to call on his intended, but he sought answers that he doubted he'd find at the keep.

After securing a room at The Dozing Stag for an undetermined length of time, Logan had exited the inn and spied a vision of such unexpected comeliness, his lungs stalled. And when his gaze collided with hers...

He knew.

Even before his attention locked on the Luckenbooth brooch, he *knew* she was Mayra Findlay—tall, fair, and blue-eyed like her sire, but with her mum's oval face, delicate bones, and bowed lips.

Never before had he experienced such a powerful and instant response to a woman.

And given her rosy cheeks and dazed expression, she'd been every bit as awestruck.

Either that or she was a promiscuous piece, practiced at snaring men with her guise of false innocence.

He skewed his mouth sideways a fraction.

How jaded and pessimistic he'd become, all because Da had married a wanton, only to learn her true character too late.

Not all women were cunning, manipulative bits like Rodena.

For the briefest instant—not more than a heartbeat really—Logan had almost told Mayra the truth. That this very day, *she* brought him to Glenliesh Village.

Or rather, seeking news of her had drawn him.

He'd opened his mouth to tell her, but unexpected and inexplicable fear of her reaction kept him mute.

What if her present fascination turned to contempt or scorn?

He still must wed her, willing or not, and he far preferred the former.

Instead, he'd held fast to his hastily-contrived plan: to poke around, and then contemplate his best course, depending on what he unearthed. He was fairly confident no one here would know of Coburn's kinship to him, so pretending to be his cousin shouldn't cause any issues.

Certainly, he didn't expect to encounter Mayra within an hour of arriving, nor could he have predicted his overwhelming reaction when he did. Even now, his jumbled thoughts caroused around in his mind, and his unruly member lay heavy and aching against his thigh.

Fine bloody time to don *Sassenach* garb.

A kilt would've saved him a great deal of mortification, but someone was sure to have recognized the Rutherford cerulean and scarlet plaid. Bending his knee and angling his leg forward, he prayed Mayra didn't notice his arousal, as he unwisely permitted himself another languid perusal of her.

Enchanting didn't begin to describe Mayra.

Even the freckles dotting her upturned nose, her faintly lopsided smile, and a small scar over her right eyebrow charmed in a precocious, elfin way. And she possessed the most unusual voice. Uncommonly low and rich for a woman, her husky brogue wrapped around his senses, bewitching and ensnaring him.

What did her laugh sound like?

Her cries of passion?

Deep and sultry like her voice?

Gettin' miles ahead of yerself there, auld chap.

Nevertheless, his manhood jerked in appreciation.

Damned intractable thing. Worse than an undisciplined pup.

Logan scrutinized her, trying to read her expression and gauge her thoughts.

No calculating or shrewdness shadowed Mayra's guileless blue gaze, and he relaxed the merest bit.

He'd stared into those wide eyes long ago, nearly two decades, before thick sable lashes framed them below winged, fawn-colored brows. His hungry gaze raked over her creamy skin, slightly turned up berry-pink mouth, dainty yet strong chin, and her hair.

Och, what magnificent hair.

The bald bairn now boasted a glorious halo of moon-spun tendrils, partially hidden beneath an atrocious straw hat with the ugliest—*what was that ghastly color?*—ribbon he'd ever seen. Her arisaid's bright hues complemented her coloring, unlike the simple woolen gown of an indistinguishable shade somewhere between tree bark and muddy riverbank brown.

She wasn't exactly attired in the first stare of fashion, yet she didn't seem ashamed or self-conscious of her clothing. Truthfully, he'd expected to find her wearing the finest English garments money could buy, as his stepmum was wont to do.

He angled his head and folded his arms.

That he recognized Mayra also flabbergasted him.

How many years since he'd last seen her?

Ten?

No, more.

The shy, awkward, rickle-a-bones lassie he'd last seen had blossomed into a rare and exquisite woman. After holding that tempting armful scant moments before, he almost hurled his plans into the tosspot.

What difference did it make if she knew who he was now?

She would soon enough in any event.

Roderick Findlay's words—words Logan hadn't recalled until this moment—echoed in his head.

"Court her."

~

I hope you enjoyed this free preview of
TO LOVE A HIGHLAND LAIRD
Book 1
Heart of a Scot Series

From the Desk of Collette Cameron®

Dearest Reader,

Gregor McTavish had to wait the longest of any of my characters to have his story told. I first introduced him in *The Highlander's Heiress*, and he made many appearances in the other *Highland Heather Romancing a Scot: Castle Brides* Series books. Initially, I planned on him marrying Lily Ellsworth, sister to my heroine in *Triumph and Treasure*, but something kept niggling at me that she wasn't quite right for Gregor.

Then Sarah's character introduced herself to me one day, and the more I got to know her, the more I became convinced she was perfect for Gregor. She's independent and intelligent —a woman who doesn't trust easily. But Gregor is just the man to teach her to trust again.

I know that the Scots didn't celebrate Christmas for centuries in Scotland, but as this story is set in Regency England, Gregor gets introduced to many Christmas traditions. I hope you enjoy reading his and Sarah's story and that you'll be intrigued enough to read the other books in the Highland Heather Romancing a Scot: Castle Brides Series.

Many of the characters in this series also appear in The Honorable Rogues® series. You can read the first chapters of all my books for free at **collettecameronbooks.com**.

Hugs,
Collette Cameron®

If you haven't joined Collette's exclusive mailing list click on QR image to sign up! You'll get access to exclusive content, sneak peeks, contests, giveaways, and more...
(P.S. No spam!)

https://collettecameronbooks.com/freegift

Collette loves to hear from readers.
You can contact her via her website: collettecameronbooks.com.
Or email her directly at collette@collettecameronbooks.com.

You can also follow Collette on social media:
Facebook: https://www.-facebook.com/ColletteCameronNovels/
Instagram: https://instagram.com/collettecameronauthor/
Goodreads: https://www.goodreads.com/collettecameron
Book Bub: https://www.bookbub.com/authors/collette-cameron

Pinterest: http://www.pinterest.com/colletteauthor/
YouTube: https://www.youtube.com/@ColletteCamero-
nAuthor

Giggles are Guaranteed
Collette's Cheris Reader Group

https://www.facebook.com/groups/CollettesCheris/

If you love to chat about all things romance-book related and enjoy taking part in fun and engaging live events, contests, and giveaways join **Collette's Chèris VIP Reader Group, https://www.facebook.com/groups/CollettesCheris/,** my exclusive private book group on Facebook.

Giggles are guaranteed!

Hope to see you there,
Collette Cameron®

COLLETTE CAMERON®

USA Today Bestselling author Collette Cameron® is renowned for her captivating, humorous, and heartwarming Scottish and Regency historical romance novels. With over 65 published titles, over 1.6 million books sold around the world, and multiple writing awards to her credit, Collette is a well-known author in the world of historical romance.

Readers love her witty and relatable characters including daring rogues, dashing scoundrels, and the strong and spirited heroines who capture their hearts. From the rugged highlands to the refined drawing rooms of Regency England, Collette's novels will transport you to another time and place, where love and adventure are just a page away.

Collette's Sweet-to-Spicy Timeless Romances® are the perfect escape for readers looking for romantic escape, poignant inspiration, engaging humor, and entertaining stories.

Based in the Pacific Northwest, Collette is surrounded by the lush greenery and rainy skies that inspire her writing. She dreams of one day splitting her time between the Pacific Northwest and Scotland. In the meantime, she indulges in her love of all things cobalt blue, dachshunds, chocolate, and of course, crafting her next historical romance.

Blue Rose Romance® LLC
collette@collettecameronbooks.com
collettecameronbooks.com

SEDUCTIVE SCOUNDRELS
A Sensual Marriage of Convenience
Regency Historical Romance

A Diamond for a Duke — Book 1

Only a Duke Would Dare — Book 2

A December with a Duke — Book 3

What Would a Duke Do? — Book 4

Wooed by a Wicked Duke — Book 5

Duchess of His Heart — Book 6

Never Dance with a Duke — Book 7

Wedding Her Christmas Duke — Book 8

The Debutante and the Duke — Book 9

Loved by a Dangerous Duke — Book 10

How to Win a Duke's Heart — Book 11

When a Duke Desires a Lass — Book 12

My Dearest Duke — Book 13

❧

FOR THE LOVE OF AN EARL (Wicked Earls' Club)
A Humorous Aristocrat and Wallflower
Regency Romance Adventure

Earl of Wainthorpe — Book 1

Earl of Scarborough — Book 2

Earl of Keyworth — Book 3

Earl of Renshaw — Book 4

❧

HEART OF A SCOT

A Passionate Enemies to Lovers

Scottish Highlander Historical Mystery

Romance Adventure

To Love a Highland Laird — Book 1

To Redeem a Highland Rogue — Book 2

To Seduce a Highland Scoundrel — Book 3

To Woo a Highland Warrior — Book 4

To Enchant a Highland Earl — Book 5

To Defy a Highland Duke — Book 6

To Marry a Highland Marauder — Book 7

To Bargain with a Highland Buccaneer — Book 8

A Christmas Kiss for the Highlander — Book 9

HIGHLAND HEATHER ROMANCING A SCOT: CASTLE BRIDES

A Passionate Enemies to Lovers Second Chance

Scottish Highlander Mystery Romance

Heart of a Highlander — Prequel

The Viscount's Vow — Book 1

The Highlander's Heiress — Book 2

The Earl's Enticement — Book 3

Triumph and Treasure — Book 4

Virtue and Valor — Book 5

Heartbreak and Honor — Book

Scandal's Splendor — Book 7

**A Second Chance Redeemable Rogue
and Wallflower Regency Romance**

A Kiss for a Rogue — Book 1

A Bride for a Rogue — Book 2

A Rogue's Scandalous Wish — Book 3

To Capture a Rogue's Heart — Book 4

The Rogue and the Wallflower — Book 5

A Rose for a Rogue — Book 6

'Twas the Rogue Before Christmas — Book 7

A Rogue Worth the Risk — Book 8